THE DARKENING PATH
BOOK TWO

SIMON AND FLORA are flung into the dangerous world of the Broken Kingdom. The Broken King himself grows madder by the day, his edicts more frightening, his whims more deadly. Whilst Anna and Johnny's lives are in danger, the kingdoms stand on the edge of war.

What is the king's daughter plotting? How far will the loyalty of the Knight of the Swan stretch? And who, exactly, is Pike?

Can Simon and Flora rescue their siblings and escape before the collapse of a throne and the outbreak of a terrible conflict? Find out in the second volume of *The Darkening Path*.

ABOUT THE AUTHOR

PHILIP WOMACK was educated at Lancing and
Oriel College, Oxford. *The Broken King* is his third
novel for children. *The Other Book* and *The Liberators*
were critically acclaimed and won him comparisons
to Alan Garner, John Masefield and M R James.

Philip is a Fellow at First Story, currently being
Writer in Residence at St Augustine's C of E High
School in Kilburn. He lives in London.

THE DARKENING PATH
BOOK ONE

THE
BROKEN
KING

Philip Womack

troika books

Published by TROIKA BOOKS

First published 2014

Troika Books

Well House, Green Lane, Ardleigh CO7 7PD, UK

www.troikabooks.com

Text copyright © Philip Womack 2014

A CIP catalogue record for this book is available
from the British Library

ISBN 978-1-909991-00-2

1 2 3 4 5 6 7 8 9 10

Printed in Poland

CONTENTS

Dauntless the slug-horn to my lips I set
And blew. 'Childe Roland to the Dark Tower came.'

From *Childe Roland to the Dark Tower Came*
by Robert Browning

I will remember this tree
With this dazzle of sun and shadow.

From *The Dark Tower*
by Louis MacNeice

Chapter One

I Call
The Broken King

SIMON WATCHED HIS parents drive away, his head throbbing and his heart heavy as the fading light of the late evening summer sun filled the front garden of the cottage.

'Look after Anna!' his father called out of the car window. His mother waved, smart in her old evening dress.

Then the car turned the corner, and Simon watched after them as they trundled down the drive leading to the cliffs, with the beach below and the grey vastness of the sea beyond. Silver lights were forming in the waves, in the shapes of birds, horses, deer.

Simon went back inside. His little sister Anna was perched on the stairs. She sprang up, and ran into the sitting room. The first thing she did was turn on the sound system and put on a pop song that Simon particularly hated.

'Look after her,' Dad said, thought Simon. *What does he know? She doesn't need looking after.* He passed the door to the sitting room and glanced in to see her jumping up and down, tunelessly singing the words to the song. *She's perfectly happy*, he thought.

Sighing, he pushed on to the kitchen, where his mother's laptop sat on the table, and logged on to a social network. There was nothing new. His friends from his old school were all on holiday. He hadn't made any new ones round here yet. He put his earphones in and selected one of his favourite tracks, trying to block out Anna's noise. He'd saved up for the music player. He hadn't been allowed a laptop – not after what had happened to his family. It was the only thing he had left from his life in London, after Dad had lost his job, and they'd come to live here in this rented cottage.

'Come and dance!'

It was Anna, next to him, tugging at his sleeve. His head throbbed more. He took out one of the earphones.

'Leave me alone,' he said quietly.

Anna ran back into the sitting room and started the song again from the beginning.

Filled with sudden fury, Simon got off the stool and stormed out of the kitchen.

'Turn it down, Anna,' he demanded, moving towards her.

She turned it up louder.

Simon tore out his other earphone. 'Anna! I said, turn it down!'

But it had no effect on her. Giggling, she turned her back on Simon, twisted the dial right up to near the top. The noise was enormous. It thudded in Simon's mind, making his head throb worse.

'Why do you always have to be so annoying?' Simon pushed past her and managed to switch off the music system. The silence rang around them.

'Why don't you ever do what I want?' replied Anna, turning it on again. 'We always do what you want, never what I want.'

That's totally not true, thought Simon. He seemed to spend his life giving in to his sister. 'I've got a headache! It really hurts! You just don't care about anyone except yourself!'

Anna stuck her tongue out and started doing a dance. 'Your songs are stupid anyway,' she said. 'You only listen to all that boring stuff.' She made a grab for his music player, but Simon held it out of her reach. Anna jiggled around. 'My favourite programme's

on!' she said, and made for the TV. Soon its light and sound were competing with the music. Simon closed his eyes and grimaced.

He remembered something that would frighten her. He rummaged about in the books on the shelf. There were some fairy stories there, things they'd been read as little children, in their other lives, before they'd moved and everything changed. 'You know what happens to little girls who annoy their brothers?' asked Simon. He picked up one of the books. It was called *In the Land of the Broken King*.

'I don't care,' mocked Anna, swishing around the room. The noise was building, higher and higher, voices blaring and beats thumping. It was getting too much for Simon.

Simon could feel the anger bubbling up inside him. He wanted to scream at her. He wanted to be with his friends. He wanted to be on the sea, in the desert, at the North Pole. Anywhere but here with his annoying little sister.

'You know the rhyme, don't you?' said Simon, turning down the TV. 'You remember it, from when we were little? You remember how scary it was?' *The illustrations in particular,* he thought. In the whole book there was never a picture of the Broken

King himself; there were just empty, desolate spaces, full of small figures struggling against the wind, and black glass towers rearing into the sky, full of strange lights.

Snorting with laughter, Anna pushed the volume button on the TV remote louder again. It was a game show, with lots of bleeping sounds and calls from the audience. Simon didn't understand why on earth Anna could be interested in it.

Anna was now bouncing up and down on the sofa, near the cabinet where his parents' few remaining bits of china were kept by a tall glass vase full of tulips.

'Anna, stop! You'll break something!'

Simon opened the book. *It's in here somewhere*, he thought. *The rhyme for getting rid of annoying siblings.* A shadow crossed his mind, and he blinked. *Why did I think of it now?* he wondered. He didn't know. It had come to him out of some deep memory. *It'll scare her, for sure, and that's all I want to do. Scare her, so she'll be quiet and leave me alone.*

'I don't care! I don't care!' shouted Anna joyfully, bouncing in time to the music, each word thudding with the beat.

'I'll call Mum and Dad!' said Simon, knowing that wouldn't work.

'Don't care! Don't care!' She jumped and fell, and with her elbow managed to knock over the vase. The glass shattered, and red petals shone wetly on the carpet.

'I'll call the police!' He waited for the effect.

But it made no difference. Anna, doubled up, was rolling around on the floor. 'Silly old Simon! Smelly old Simon!'

Simon ground his teeth.

She leaped up, made another grab for his music player, and tore it from his grasp. She put it into her ears and started doing a stupid dance.

'Give it back! Give that back!' He snatched for it, but she jumped out of his reach.

'Oh, I'm Simon. I'm so clever. I like really boring music!' Anna was striking a pose and laughing.

That's it, thought Simon. He made to grab the music player from her hand. They tussled over it – Simon pulled hard, and Anna pulled back harder. She slipped, the player flew up into the air and fell right into the pool of water that the vase had made.

Simon watched helplessly as the screen went a funny colour.

'You've broken it!' he said. He lifted it up from the water and pressed its buttons. The screen remained

a dull purple. He flung it aside in rage.

'Don't care! Don't care!' shouted Anna.

Outside the sun was almost touching the sea. *Right*, he thought. *I'll teach you a lesson.* Anger was twisting inside his belly. *I'll go round the room and I'll pretend to be the Broken King and I'll give you the fright of your life.*

It was then that he found the rhyme. The book fell open to the right page. He glanced over it.

Three times and the Broken King will take her.

The poem looked different from how he remembered it. *That's because it's been so long since I read it*, he thought. He looked at the book in his hands. The illustrations gave him the shivers.

Don't be silly. It's just a book.

'Anna! I'm going to do it. I'm going to call him. I'm going to call the Broken King and he's going to take you away!' *I'll show her*, he thought.

The sun hovered on the horizon. Anna shrieked, 'I'm not scared of him any more!' The television blared.

Simon gritted his jaw and took a deep breath. *Now, what did you have to do?* he wondered. *It was three times round the room, anti-clockwise. Widdershins, they called it in the book. Then, just as the sun sets, I'll frighten her.*

'I'm starting!' He held the book out open on the

page, and stalked round the room once, backwards, tripping over one of Anna's dolls and nearly stepping on the remote control. Anna was laughing hysterically in the middle of the carpet, rolling from side to side and waving her arms around.

Simon beat his foot on the ground in time to his chanting. He intoned, heavily, loudly.

'I call the Broken King.

Walk backwards thrice in a ring.'

Anna gurgled with laughter. 'Simon, Simon, smelly old Simon!'

He carried on pacing quickly.

The sun was sinking, the room filling with twilight. Shadows slid around the edges of the walls.

It was almost as if he wasn't in control of himself. He found himself speaking the words of the poem without thinking about them.

'He'll come in blinding light.

He'll wrap you in the night.'

Simon was barely aware of the movement of his body. A buzzing was filling his mind. His limbs felt light and strange, his voice as if it was coming from somewhere that wasn't his own throat. It was like some other power had taken over him. He couldn't stop now, even if he'd wanted to.

'*Before the start of day*
The Broken King will take you away!'

He finished by the sofa, the last syllable drowned by the chorus of Anna's pop song. The sun's rays pulled back from the room, and everything darkened.

Simon suddenly felt silly. *Why would I want to scare her?* he thought and paused.

Anna was lying on her back, shaking with laughter. Another song was playing. Simon reached over behind the sofa to turn it off, then picked up the remote and switched the TV off too. Its red light gleamed. He lit a standing lamp, and was grateful for the glow it cast.

Simon was shivering. The buzzing noise in his mind gradually dimmed, and left him with nothing but his headache. He looked at Anna, who was now still, and felt a sudden rush of love for his sister. She sat up and regarded him reproachfully.

'Come on now, Anna. It's time for bed,' he said gently. 'Nothing's going to get you.'

'Don't want to go to bed!' she squealed. 'I want ice cream!'

Irritation swarmed through Simon. He clenched his teeth and pushed it down. *She is my little sister*, he thought. He reached out to her.

She stopped squealing, looked up at him, and smiled.

'Come on, you silly thing,' said Simon softly.

Then the shadow passed over his mind again, and Simon heard a sound like a horn blowing. It was so loud he had to cover his ears. It grew louder and louder until he had to kneel down on the floor, as if it was physically battering him.

Light filled the room, bright and white. Something was shaking. The moon, bright and quivering. Somewhere doors were opening, and things were sliding through. Shadows stealing towards them. A sword, shining and cruel. Shapes flitting through the night. Shapes like humans – looming, tall – reaching towards Anna.

What's going on? thought Simon, panicking. *It can't be. It can't be the Broken King.*

But there was somebody standing over Anna, a dark shape, and it was holding a sword.

Simon tried to move but the force of the sound prevented him. He heard Anna screaming, and called her name. In the light he saw a white face and teeth gleaming.

He forced himself forwards. The figure laid hold of Anna's arm.

'Simon!' she called. 'Help me!'

Summoning all his strength, Simon crawled on his hands and knees towards Anna. The sound of the horn became unbearable. He put his hands to his ears once more.

The figure hauled Anna up from the ground, and stepped back into the blinding light.

'Simon! Simon!' Her voice was faint now. Simon held a hand in front of his eyes. He saw the figure bow and smile, and heard Anna call his name again.

Light glinted off the steel of the sword, and the figure turned and Anna screamed and Simon ran towards her and then there was nothing.

Simon fell to the floor, and saw that there was blood on his hand from where he'd taken it away from his ear, and then he slipped down into darkness.

When he woke up, he was in his bed, and it was just before dawn. His mind was blank and empty. He sat up quickly, feeling that something was wrong.

Something, some noise, drew him to the window. Was that movement outside in the shrubs, in the bracken?

The fat moon jolted his memory. Fear gripped his heart.

Anna! He remembered everything in a dizzying rush. He'd said that rhyme, intoned it like a spell, and then there had been that noise, that light, that . . . man.

A dream, he thought. He scolded himself for being stupid. It was only a dream. *I'll check on her. I'll have a look in Anna's room.* He pinched himself, and felt the sharp pain.

But had he been dreaming? Terror eased its way slowly through his bones.

She'll be in her bed, thought Simon. *She'll be curled up under her duvet with her stupid teddy bear and I'll wake her up and she'll jump out of bed and we'll go and watch her stupid programme on TV and it will all be OK.*

He crept on to the small landing. Nothing creaked. There were five doors – one to his parents' room, which was firmly closed; one to the bathroom, which was open; one to an airing cupboard; and his own and his sister's, which were ajar.

Gritting his teeth, he tiptoed toward Anna's room. Her name was spelled out on it in rainbow letters. He heard a snore coming from his parents' room. They were back, then.

He pushed Anna's door further open, gently. The

room wasn't very big. There was a small blue chest of drawers with a mirror and a mess of toys on it. There was an open wardrobe with sparkly dresses poking out of it. There was her bed. The window was shut.

The duvet was scrumpled up. He felt relief wash through him. She was there. He skipped over to the bed and pulled at the duvet, about to let out a laugh, tickle her, ruffle her hair.

A scatter of teddies fell to the floor.

There was no sign of Anna.

Simon felt his heart begin to beat faster. It *had* happened. It had actually happened. That nursery rhyme. It wasn't a rhyme at all. It was a spell of some kind. It had to be. He'd said it, as the sun was setting, and the Broken King had come to get her. Just as Simon had wanted.

He slapped his forehead. It was unbelievable. How could it be true? She must be somewhere else in the house.

A sudden thought struck him, and he scuttled across the landing into his room, thinking she might have sneaked in there to surprise him. She liked to come and see him in the mornings sometimes.

But she wasn't there. He stepped back out on to

the landing, thinking. He tiptoed over to his parents' room, and pushed open the door.

There was his father, lying on his back in his striped red and white pyjamas, snoring gently. There was his mother, on her side, her long black hair spreading down her face. There was no Anna bouncing around the bed; no Anna sitting on the floor playing with her ponies; no Anna jumping up and down asking to be allowed to watch TV.

A horrible realisation began to take hold of him. He went back into his room, sat down on his bed and put his head in his hands.

There was movement there, outside his window. Without thinking he crept downstairs. His heart was beating quickly.

Anna. Anna, is that you?

Maybe she'd gone outside in the early morning. He didn't want to call, in case he woke up his parents. They would be so angry. He would find her first, and then bring her in and pretend nothing had ever happened. Maybe she'd gone down to the cliffs.

He ran past his parents' car in the drive, down from the cottage towards the edge of the cliffs. When he got there, he paused. There was nothing. No movement. Of course it wasn't Anna. He looked

down at the blue-green hugeness of the sea.

Though he was wearing nothing but a T-shirt and a pair of boxer shorts, he did not feel the cold.

Sunlight was spreading towards him across the surface of the waves, making shapes again. A bird. A deer. A woman.

He lowered himself until he leaned against a rock, and held out his arms to the empty air. *Whoever you are*, he thought, *whatever you are, take me. Take me instead. I didn't believe it would happen. You took her away. Give her back! Take me!*

He waited.

But nothing came.

He was overwhelmed and the tears fell, one by one.

When he could cry no more, he sat on the brink of the clifftop not moving, not speaking, staring into the bright glare of the sea.

Chapter Two

THE
BIRD-DEER

SIMON HEARD THE sound of something like hooves on the path, and lifted his head up from his knees. *What could that be?* he wondered, and then was frightened. *Maybe it's what took Anna.*

He remembered wishing her away, and wiped away a tear. He wondered what had taken her. He remembered the glint of a sword, the white face and the gleaming teeth – and Anna's cry. *I should face it . . . whatever it is.* Filled with sudden resolve, he looked up.

Golden sunlight dazzled him. He could hear a low, soft noise, like someone or something breathing

quietly. There was movement, but the glare was too bright for him to see what it was. He blinked, twice, three times. His sight was all wrong and blurry.

There was a clipping sound, as if a horse were walking nearby. It was measured, gentle. *It wants me*, thought Simon suddenly. *Whatever that is, it wants me.*

Everything was gold. He shadowed his eyes with his hand and saw a mass of golden light, almost like a ball of liquid, hovering in front of him. Simon backed away, feeling heat coming from it as the mass shivered and jittered – as if made up of lots of tiny particles – and moulded itself into a shape. Or maybe, Simon thought, something had come out of it. It was difficult to tell. The golden mass wavered and flickered, like a lamp turning on and off, and then a form was standing solid and alive in front of him.

It was a tall deer with a graceful, delicate head and tiny antlers curving in towards each other, a little like the white hart in the picture above Simon's father's desk.

Simon shook his head from side to side. What he seemed to be seeing could not be possible. On each of the deer's flanks were what looked like folded

wings, as iridescent and bright and multi-coloured as a peacock's feathers. As Simon watched, the deer lightly flicked its wings in and out, just like a bird.

Simon hugged himself and felt sweat bead on his forehead. The dew on the grass around the deer was steaming. *But it isn't a deer, is it?* he thought. *It's a bird-deer.*

The most strange thing about it was that sitting on the back of the bird-deer was a woman – at least, that was the word which sprang to Simon's mind, but she was like no one that Simon had ever seen.

Either she was cased in metal, or she was made from pure, golden light. Her hair fell in long golden waves down the back of her neck. Simon watched her stroke the bird-deer's head in-between its ears, as Simon would a dog. The bird-deer stamped its foot daintily and sniffed, bending its head slightly and regarding Simon with inquisitive eyes. Simon noticed that it had no reins or bridle, and the woman didn't appear to be sitting on a saddle.

Simon stood as still as he was able. It was as if a dream had come to him, out of the sky, out of the vastness of space, or slipped from the depths of his mind.

The woman on the bird-deer trotted closer to

Simon, then stopped a mere arm's length away. A power like electricity was radiating from them, and he felt hairs rise all over his body. Even so, he wanted to touch them, to make sure they were real. He reached out a flat hand to caress the animal's muzzle.

His fingers came nearer and nearer to the creature, which remained demure and elegant, its head bowed. The woman's expression was inscrutable.

Simon's hand was now within a hand's breadth of the beast. Everything else seemed to fade away. There was only the bird-deer, standing there in a halo of its own light, and the woman seated on its back, staring at Simon with no emotion at all in her eyes. He was just about to stroke the bird-deer's muzzle when pain shot through his fingers. He retracted his hand as if he'd been burned and sucked at the place where it hurt. Now Simon found he couldn't bear to look at the woman. It felt as if she could peer right into his mind and know every shameful thought he'd ever had.

That was why he knelt in the grass and bowed his head. He could not see the sky or the clouds or even the sun, but he heard the distant roaring of the sea.

Simon supposed the woman spoke. He heard her words, certainly, but they were emblazoned in his mind, like sound made out of light, as if his sight and hearing had melted together into one.

'Simon Goldhawk,' she said. 'I know where your sister is.'

A flame of happiness surged through him. 'Is she safe?' Simon dared to look up at her. *How does she know my name?* he thought briefly. *How does she know about my sister?*

'She is alive.'

She didn't say if she's safe, though, thought Simon. 'Where?'

Her brightness almost blinded him, and he looked down again. Her words had caused the beginnings of joy to flower in his heart.

'She has been taken.'

'Where?' asked Simon again, his voice cracking a little. Sweat still poured down his face. His green T-shirt was black with it.

'Into the darkness.' The woman's light flickered. The word conveyed more than simply dark. In Simon's mind it came to him weighted with pain, horror, fear and sadness. He could find no other word to explain the whole experience.

'Into the world of the Broken King. You asked, and he has taken her.'

The Broken King, thought Simon. *A name out of fairy tales, out of my childhood book. A name that is now true – and part of my world. Where*, wondered Simon, *is the land of the Broken King?*

The thought struck him again that the woman on the bird-deer might have taken Anna. He remembered the despairing landscapes that illustrated *In the Land of the Broken King*, the obsidian towers that rose into the sky, the small, hurrying figures. Was that a real place? He felt afraid, but this creature of light did not seem to fit with those images.

'Are you from him – the Broken King?'

'I am not,' she said fiercely.

The truth of it hit him like a wave. This woman was something entirely other than the Broken King and his darkness.

Simon didn't know how to continue. He searched around in his mind for something he could connect to what he knew. He found it in half-remembered Bible stories. 'Are you an angel?' he asked.

Something that might have been laughter rippled through the air.

'In a manner of speaking,' replied the woman.

Simon saw the bird-deer stamping its foot and snorting, its shining wings rustling with amusement.

'I am a messenger,' she said. 'I am from the Golden Realm. We watched you, Simon. We heard you call the Broken King. We saw your sister being taken. We have seen this before. We know what you have to do to get her back. Do you want her back, Simon Goldhawk?'

Of course I do, he thought. *More than I've ever wanted anything in my life. I've been so stupid. A nursery rhyme!* Guilt struck him fiercely. *I wanted Anna to go, wanted her to leave me alone. But now . . .* He pictured her, dancing to that awful pop song, and couldn't help smiling. *I love her. She's my sister.*

'Yes,' said Simon. 'Yes, I want her back.' He said it with as much feeling as he could muster.

'Good,' said the woman, as if satisfied. 'She is a prisoner. The Broken King keeps her.'

'How can I get to her?' Simon asked. The thought that Anna was being held captive caused him sharp pain.

'You will have to journey far to bring her back. But she is not far away at all.'

That didn't make sense. Far, but not far at all . . . Another thought came to him, cutting through,

sharp and clear. His parents. How could he leave his parents? Mum, sitting in front of her laptop, endlessly tapping away. Dad, head in his hands, those boxes and books he never opened, those rejection letters piling up in the bin.

The woman understood Simon without him saying anything. 'We will arrange matters here . . . You must leave today. The Broken King's emissaries know you already. Keep your eyes open. There are many dangers. You must be alert, alive to everything. You will find help in places you don't expect. And what is more . . .'

The voice stopped, and Simon detected the faintest hint of a crease appearing on the woman's forehead. She seemed to reconsider something, and stayed silent. The bird-deer flared its nostrils and raised its left foreleg. It seemed to be looking at him, challenging him, daring him.

Simon was stung into speaking. 'How do I know you are who you say you are? How do I know you're not from – him? The Broken King? You say you're from the Golden Realm – I don't even know what that means! I don't know what's going on!' The strangeness of it was taking hold of him. He felt he'd become a little boy again. He shook his head

from side to side, as if to get rid of what he was seeing, to quell the troubling currents in his mind.

'You will see,' said the woman.

'How will I know where to go?' asked Simon. He was swirling, dizzied.

'I will wait for you. Towards eight, I will be by the oak tree behind the field to the north. I will take you to where you will find a way forward.'

'But my parents . . .'

'I will resolve it,' she said.

What did she mean? What would she do to them? He felt trapped, bewildered. 'Anna,' said Simon. 'What will happen to her? I mean, if I don't rescue her.'

Silence. Only heat came from the woman and the bird-deer.

And then a message. In his mind he saw Anna, alone, crouched in the corner of a dark room, a high window above her looking out on to nothing. Her face was blank. He felt sadness, loneliness, emptiness. Something moved in the shadows. Something that made Simon's gut twist in fear. He gasped in horror as the thing advanced towards Anna, as she shrank back further, unable to defend herself . . .

'Stop! Stop it!' called Simon.

He watched as Anna put her arms up in front of

her face, and the blackness began to encroach upon her . . .

The vision disappeared. He was left panting, fearful. He backed away on to his haunches.

'That has not happened yet,' said the woman. 'But it might. It lies there, in her future, if you do not find her.'

Simon understood. If he did not go now, he would never see Anna again. He would have left his sister to a terrible fate, and all because of a whim; because he'd felt angry; because he'd had a headache; because she'd broken his music player. A coil of guilt wound through him.

The woman wheeled the bird-deer's head suddenly towards the sea. As she turned, Simon cooled down, feeling relieved. He ran a finger round the inside of his T-shirt. He was soaked in perspiration.

Then the woman whipped back, and he felt something slice through the air and strike him on the cheek. He yelped with pain and held his hand to his face.

'That is for your sister,' said the woman impassively.

Simon let the tears that rose in him flow. His cheek stung like hell.

The bird-deer started to walk, and then to run, its spindly legs gathering speed. The woman leaned in, her body lying along the bird-deer's neck.

Against the blinding light of the sun Simon saw the silhouette of the woman on the bird-deer, its wings stretched out and beating, bigger than an eagle's. He felt the slight breeze of disturbed air on his face.

At the edge of his sight he sensed his next-door neighbour, Francis Weston, waving hello as he took his dog past the end of the drive to the beach. A swan glided down to land on the surface of the pond nearby.

He watched the woman on the bird-deer fly away, out across the sea above the horizon, and into the sun.

Chapter Three

TREE,
STONE, CIRCLE

SIMON RAN BACK into the house. As he went past the age-blackened mirror that hung in the hallway he couldn't help stopping to look into it.

On his face there was a large welt, raised and swollen. He put his finger to his cheek and brought it away, wincing with the pain. His mind was racing. There wasn't much time till eight, and he had to prepare for a journey to somewhere that he hadn't even believed existed, that he'd seen only in the pages of a story book.

This is ridiculous, he thought.

But the welt on his cheek told him otherwise.

Then he thought of his parents. He tiptoed back upstairs, heart fluttering, and listened at their door. He could still hear the faint snores of his father. They must have got back round three and gone straight to bed without checking on Anna. It was a Saturday, so they'd probably be asleep for a bit longer. But how on earth would he explain it all to them when they woke up?

What took Anna? he thought. *And what woke me up? The moon*, he remembered, *bright and round and fat. The moon – and the shadow.* He shivered.

Something hardened in him when he looked into Anna's bedroom and saw her teddies lying on the floor. *I'll pack now*, he thought. *I'll follow the golden woman, find Anna. The Broken King* . . . It was just a rhyme, after all, how could it be frightening? He tried to remember what else the rhyme said – were there more verses to the poem he'd read?

He went into the sitting room and looked through *In the Land of The Broken King*, but couldn't find any more verses. In fact, the words on the page seemed different now. He put the book away, confused. Then he tiptoed back upstairs, delved under his bed and found the shoebox that he kept there. It was full of charity bracelets, postcards, ticket stubs, a few printed-out emails, and a porcupine spine that Anna

had picked up off the ground when they were on holiday in Italy.

It was the only thing she'd ever given him. He put the porcupine spine in his pocket, and then he set about packing. *I didn't even ask how long I would be gone*, he thought. He glanced outside his window as he went past it, and saw that a swan had landed by the end of the drive, and was pacing up and down, rearing its snaky head.

Rooting in his wardrobe, he found a big rucksack already packed with bits left over from previous trips he didn't bother looking at, and a small pop-up tent. He added a sleeping bag to the rucksack, along with a jumper, a pair of jeans, and a first aid kit from the bathroom, then found a torch and some batteries.

Hefting it on to his shoulder, he went downstairs into the kitchen. Water, apples, bread. Tinned tomatoes? A knife? It was nearly eight o'clock. He had a moment of panic. Should he bring his phone? Would he need it? He almost laughed. Did they get reception in the land of the Broken King?

Simon put the rucksack down by the door and hugged himself as he looked out. He saw that the swan was now in the garden, waddling up to the open kitchen door.

What should he do now? Wake his parents up? Wait for a sign from the messenger?

He jumped, startled by the sound of the swan, which was poking its head around the door and hissing at him. *They can break your arm*, thought Simon. *That's what everyone says, isn't it? And worse . . . But what on earth is it doing here?* The swan reared its wings, its serpentine neck waving.

It's going to attack me! Simon realised. He looked around wildly for something to throw at it. His hand closed on a cheese grater. The swan beat its wings and jabbed its beak forwards.

Simon threw the cheese grater. It clattered, uselessly, by the door, and the swan lunged. *Oh no!* thought Simon. He looked around for anything else to defend himself with, but could only find an empty bowl, which he threw anyway. It missed and fell, rolling away into a corner.

The swan lurched forwards, hissing, and jabbed in Simon's direction. Simon jumped backwards to the kitchen door, slipping, and grabbed on to the table. He managed to steady himself as the swan swung back for another attack. Simon ducked behind the table, using it as a barrier, and wildly scrabbled around him for something – anything – to use in defence.

Simon braced himself to beat off the swan with his arms alone, but as the swan arced its beak, he saw the mad fury in the swan's eyes and felt the atmosphere in the room change.

His heart leaped. The messenger was there. He recognised that warmth. The golden light from before returned and bathed the room.

Simon gasped. The swan, still poised for attack, was now a man – tall, white-skinned and naked. His expression was fierce and cold, and his black hair hung around his pale face, his blue eyes glaring at Simon.

And then he was a swan again. A flare shot out from the light towards it. The swan hissed and waddled away, taking flight clumsily from the garden path. The golden light around Simon intensified, and the woman on the bird-deer appeared there in the kitchen.

Simon, panting, all but collapsed on to a chair. He wiped his forehead with his forearm.

'The Knight of the Swan,' the messenger said simply.

'Why is he here?' asked Simon, fearful. Looking out, he saw the swan was now nothing more than a dot in the sky.

'A servant of the Broken King. His name is Sir Mark. I am glad that you have seen him. You will know now to avoid him.' The bird-deer whinnied, fluttered its wings and flared its nostrils, as if to show disgust. 'We must go now. If we do not, then he will return, and I do not know what – or who – he will return with.'

'My parents!' said Simon, louder than he'd wanted to. He realised they must be awake now, with the swan and all the noise it had made. He looked manically around at the items strewn around the kitchen. What if his parents came downstairs now? What would they say? How would he explain about Anna?

'The knight will be off to tell his master the king about this meeting,' said the woman. 'We must leave now.'

Simon was suddenly filled with resistance. *I'm going mad*, he thought. *I must be. Anna's upstairs, probably sleeping there in Mum and Dad's bed. This is all a dream. A really weird, really vivid dream.*

'No!' he shouted. 'I don't believe you. You're not real.' A tear came down his cheek. 'I know you're not real! I'm going to close my eyes and when I open them you won't be there.'

He screwed his eyes tightly shut, and counted

loudly to fifteen. But even as he opened them, he knew that the woman on the bird-deer would still be there.

And she was, casting her golden light on the kitchen table and the sink and the clock that always told the wrong time, and Anna's wellington boots which sat by the kitchen door – pink and polka-dotted, one toppled over on to its side.

The messenger looked displeased for a second, then her face set into its usual impassive mask.

'I said I will arrange matters.' The bird-deer pawed the ground haughtily. 'Leave the house.'

Simon, backing away and more than a little frightened by the steel in her voice, slipped out of the kitchen door. He turned on the threshold and peered back in.

The messenger was holding her arms out. Once more it struck Simon that the messenger and the bird-deer seemed to be made of the same substance. Maybe, somehow, they were even the same being. But then she dismounted, and walked to one side of the room, and the bird-deer trotted over to the other. Simon watched them pace in opposite directions, trailing golden light behind them. The light stayed where they passed, like a rope made of gold which hung in the air.

The woman and the bird-deer met by the kitchen door. Their light was now much dimmer; Simon could hardly see the outline of the woman, and the bird-deer's glossy feathers had lost their sheen.

They bowed to each other, then the woman lightly mounted again, and trotted out to where Simon was standing, his mouth open in awe.

The whole house was now glowing with golden light, as if the sun's rays were covering it entirely. It shimmered. *As if it's not quite there. As if it's a reflection in a pool of water that's been disturbed by a pebble,* thought Simon.

Simon's neighbour, Francis Weston, was walking back up past the house. *Oh no,* thought Simon. *He'll see it, and he'll wonder what's going on, and he'll see me and the bird-deer . . .*

Francis's dog sniffed at the edge of the drive, but Francis pressed on, not even looking in the direction of the house. The dog whimpered, then pattered after his owner.

Simon relaxed. A little.

'We have put the house into a holding place,' said the woman, reading Simon's mind. 'It is somewhere else. Nobody walking past will be able to see it as it is. They will not want to come here.

The light deflects and confuses. People will forget why they came, and will not wonder where you or your family are.'

'What about my parents?' Simon ran towards the house, but the woman and the bird-deer were in his way, and he felt afraid of pushing past them.

'Your parents have been put into deep sleep. If you succeed and bring Anna back, they will not know that anything has happened at all. Time . . . stretches differently there and here. If you do not . . .'

'What?' asked Simon, trembling.

The woman looked troubled for a second. 'You can come back here. Your house will return and they will wake up again. But while you will remember Anna, they won't.'

'And if I . . . die?'

'They will not know that you or Anna ever existed.'

So that was it, then. He conquered every last shred of doubt inside himself. He had to go, or he and Anna would have nothing: no home, no family, no future. He took one last look around at the garden, and then back at the messenger.

She started off, the bird-deer's head pointed away from Simon, and Simon, helplessly, followed with

the hastily packed rucksack on his back. He turned round to look at the cottage, glowing and golden.

I didn't even say goodbye to my parents, he thought.

As he watched, the light dimmed, and then it was as if his house had never been there.

He felt the pull of the woman and the bird-deer, and tore himself away.

They went on, a little faster than Simon could manage without running from time to time, through a small copse that descended a gentle hill into a valley where a stream ran. As the bird-deer passed through the waters, Simon could have sworn that they steamed a little.

He panted to keep up with them. They passed a couple of hikers who smiled at Simon but made no sign of wonder. *They can't see her*, thought Simon, and once again wondered if he was going mad.

After almost an hour he had to stop. He bent over, his whole body layered in sweat, his chest heaving. He guzzled down an entire bottle of water, and had a good look around. He didn't recognise where they were any more. He could tell they'd been heading north, and figured that the hills around them must be the South Downs.

The messenger stopped and turned, then trotted

back to him. The bird-deer nuzzled him. This time, as it touched him, instead of being shocked or hurt he felt renewed. *It must be giving me some kind of energy*, Simon thought. *Maybe it can control what kind of energy it gives out.* He gazed into the beast's mournful eyes and thought of his sister; he did not dare to look directly at the messenger.

The messenger and the bird-deer led him on and on, further into the Downs. The summer air was thick; the woods around them green and whispering. They went past countless beeches and the monstrous trunk of an ancient yew tree.

Sometimes the golden pair would gallop ahead, and Simon would feel a blissful few seconds of coolness. But there was a tug in his stomach which led him onwards, even when he couldn't see his guides, as surely as if there was a compass inside him.

They came to another stream. This one was almost dry, and the waters flowed sluggishly. The pebbles on its bed glimmered in the sunlight. The golden pair leaped across, borne by the bird-deer's wings, in one graceful arc.

Simon followed more wearily. He got his feet wet in the brook, and he had to scramble up the other side of the bank. When he reached the sweet grass

on the other side, he slumped down, and all the energy ebbed out of him.

He lay there and the messenger let him be for a while. He daydreamed, his mind full of light and shadow, fire and stone.

Soon enough the bird-deer's gentle touch on his face revived him. He smiled, got up.

But the messenger said nothing, and went on ahead once more.

They walked for another hour, more slowly now. Simon's strides were becoming heavier and heavier. They came to a small clearing. The centre of it was raised and grassy. In the middle was a stone, like a pillar, standing up by itself. The messenger and the bird-deer stopped next to it. The bird-deer lifted its muzzle haughtily and stared at Simon sideways.

Simon took a few stumbling steps towards them, then, exhausted, he slumped down by the standing stone. The woman dismounted and lay down on one side of him as the bird-deer knelt by the other. Surrounded by warmth, he fell asleep. In his dreams he saw one thing, and one thing only: Anna, crouched and alone in the darkness.

He was woken by a light that, when he tried to

open his eyes, all but blinded him. He felt the grass under him, warm and dry, and for a while he lay there on his side, his bag under his cheek. Images, confused and mysterious, danced in his mind.

'Hello?'

He heard the voice, a girl's, and thought: *Anna!*

Then he remembered. How could he have forgotten? Something poked him in the ribs and, since it didn't stop, he felt that he ought to sit up and see what it was.

'Hello?'

The voice again – definitely a female voice. He blinked. He couldn't adjust his eyes to the light of day.

'Are you all right?'

Simon blinked again and a face came into focus.

Dirty was the first word that elbowed its way into Simon's mind. *Cross* was the next. He saw long black hair falling on either side of, and obscuring most of, a face that was muddied and bleeding. A hand appeared and brushed aside a lock, revealing a pair of eyes that looked frankly and, if Simon had to put a label on it, a little challengingly at him.

'Are you all right?' repeated the girl.

Simon was feeling a little better, and rooted

around in his bag for a bottle of water. He found it and offered it to the girl, who batted it away. He shrugged, put it to his lips and glugged greedily. She was wearing quite a lot of eyeliner, Simon saw, and a blue hoodie that looked soft. Over it was a black leather jacket that was two or three sizes too big for her. She wore a skirt with little flowers on it, and tatty blue trainers with white soles.

Simon sat up, and the girl, who had been squatting, readjusted herself and dropped down next to him in the grass.

'Did you see it?' said the girl, as a bird – a rook, thought Simon – flapped out from a branch above them. The girl shrieked at the noise, and grabbed Simon's arm, then immediately composed herself.

'See what?' He put his water bottle away. 'I've got a plaster if you like . . . You need to clean yourself up.'

'Do I? Oh, well, I fell down quite a lot. It was going so quickly . . .'

Simon rummaged around and pulled out a small first aid kit.

'Here,' he said.

She held her cheek up towards him and he dabbed at it with the mineral water, then put a little drop of cream on the cut. He fiddled for a second or two

with the plaster, before managing to open it up and stick it on.

'There,' he said. 'You'd never know.' He didn't know why he said it; it was the sort of thing that people said when they put plasters on other people.

'I don't even want to think about it,' she said. 'And by the way, you haven't even asked me yet.'

'Asked you what?'

'What I was following.'

Simon felt a little nervous. He had an idea, but he didn't want to admit it. Surely the bird-deer had been for him, for him alone?

'Well, are you going to ask or aren't you? It disappeared here. Just by this stone.'

Simon spoke slowly. 'So what did you follow here?' *It can't have been my woman, my bird-deer,* he thought.

The girl's exuberance vanished. She looked away. 'Now I have to say it, it sounds so . . .' She trailed off.

'Go on.'

'It was a . . . I don't know . . . a . . .'

Simon bit his tongue. 'A deer?'

'Yes! Did you see it too?'

'A deer . . . with wings . . . and on the back of it was . . .'

'A man!'

So it hadn't been the same one, thought Simon. The lady had been only for him, and for that he felt a sense of hot gratitude.

'When did it come to you?' said Simon. 'Oh – and my name's Simon, by the way.'

'Mine's Flora. Sorry, I should have said.' She paused and flicked her hair. 'How about yours?'

Simon considered her. Could he trust her? He looked away from Flora, swallowing heavily. She was here, after all, by the stone, in the circle, and she'd seen a bird-deer. She must be all right. She must be looking for someone similar. Maybe somebody had taken her sister, or her brother, as well. And maybe she would be able to help.

Flora cut over his thoughts. 'Simon . . . Look . . . He came – I mean, the man on the deer came – after my brother – he's eighteen – he went. Or disappeared. I don't know. But the police don't . . . don't care so much about adults. Especially if they . . .' She stopped herself. 'He just . . . vanished. He was in his room. He was trying to get . . . and then . . . he wasn't. In his room.' Her voice changed. 'I love him.' The sadness trembled in her face. 'I love him and I ran away after this . . . golden vision. The man told me yesterday . . . He told me I could find Johnny. The rhyme . . . I

don't know why I said it!'

So she said it too, thought Simon. *Maybe there's something more going on here.* He put that thought aside for later. 'What about your parents?'

She sniffed. 'If you really want to know, my father's abroad and my mother's . . . with someone else. They're divorced. I go off on my own quite a lot – I told mum yesterday I was going up to friends in Scotland with no internet or phone reception. To be honest, my mother doesn't particularly care where I am. She's usually . . .' She thought of her mother, face down on the kitchen table, an empty gin bottle by her side, and decided not to say anything more. 'Well, she's got someone to look after her, anyway. So,' she said, clearing her throat, 'how about you?'

'The deer . . .' said Simon. 'Except mine was a woman. At least, she looked like a woman. And she came first after my . . . my sister . . . after she vanished.' *I won't say it*, thought Simon. *I won't say that I wished her away as well.* He looked down at the grass and saw a line of ants marching purposefully towards the trees. 'I love my sister too,' said Simon. He wiped away what he hoped Flora hadn't noticed were tears from his eyes. To cover it up, he continued, 'Do you know where we are?' He'd thought they must be

somewhere on the Downs. He didn't recognise the clearing, but he was pretty sure they'd been going steadily north.

Flora shook her head. 'I was following it – him – so blindly I didn't look at a map or anything like that. I didn't even think to bring my phone with me. Did you?'

Simon shook his head. He hadn't managed to pick it up before the swan attacked.

Flora sighed. 'Where do you live?' she asked.

Did I live, thought Simon grimly. 'Up past Limerton, in a cottage by the sea. You?'

'Moreton-on-the-Green.'

It wasn't far – the next village along from Simon to the north. 'So what do you think they were? The deer – and the people on them,' said Simon.

'I don't know,' said Flora. 'I mean, I've read about white harts before. They always come to feasts at the court of King Arthur and lead the knights on a quest.'

'So we've been led here on purpose?' said Simon.

'I suppose so,' said Flora. She stood up suddenly. 'Look – we're in a clearing in a forest. There's a stone in the middle of this circle – a standing stone. Don't you think it's possible that my brother – and

your sister – are around here somewhere? Standing stones are always a bit . . . mythical, aren't they?'

'Why here?'

'The . . . the Broken King. The entrance to his kingdom might be around here. You know.' She looked shifty. 'The nursery rhyme? I still don't think it's really true . . .'

Recognising the quiet desperation in Flora's eyes, Simon said, 'Well then, let's look.'

The clearing was not large, maybe twenty metres across. The grass was a lush, dark green. The trees around the edges were white on the underside of their leaves, apart from one tall and imposing oak, and a different tree that seemed to have sporadic clusters of long white flowers hanging from its branches.

'How shall we do it?'

Simon remembered a camping trip he'd been on at school. They'd been trained to comb the site for any rubbish before they left. He explained the system to Flora. So at first they split up, walking round in opposite directions, looking for signs of concealed entrances or track marks. Then they joined forces, and crawled across the whole area, feeling the ground for anything that might be odd. But all they

found was an old button and a pencil stub. Wanting to keep the place tidy, Simon put them in his pocket.

Simon positioned himself by a tree, needing to be alone and to think what to do next. He was mildly disgruntled when Flora came and lay next to him.

'Nothing. It's hopeless,' said Flora, yawning. 'It's all mad, anyway. I think Johnny's gone – and your sister too. I must be crazy. *We* must be crazy.'

'Don't say that. We're not going crazy. And Johnny and Anna haven't gone for good,' said Simon. He felt anger prick at his insides. He looked at Flora. She hadn't even brought any provisions with her or anything. What use was she going to be on this journey?

'I just know,' he said. 'I know we're going to find them.'

'Oh you know?' said Flora. 'You think you can just up and leave your family and everything because you know? How do you know?'

'Well, I was quite happy on my own. I didn't ask you to come and annoy me. Did your messenger tell you anything? About the Broken King or the Golden Realm?"

'And what were you going to do? Those people on the deer – they've gone! Broken Kingdom, Broken

King, Golden Realm – whoever heard of such things, apart from in stories. We're both mad. Mad with grief, probably. It's a recognisable thing, I expect. I bet you can read about it in medical journals. Delusions. Psychosis. Oh God, I'm actually going mad. As if everything else wasn't bad enough –'

'Shut up!' said Simon savagely. 'Shut up!' He was astonished by the force of his own voice. He was breathing heavily. He wiped away sweat from his cheek. Looking up, he was about to apologise, when Flora spoke.

'Wait,' she said. Her tone had changed. It was sharper, focused. She was looking intently over Simon's shoulder.

'What is it?'

'We've searched all around the clearing and found nothing.'

'I know that,' he said, a little of his anger released.

'But maybe we're looking in the wrong place.'

'What do you mean?' Simon replied, gritting his teeth together. His face had reddened and his eyes were wet.

Flora pointed upwards.

There was something hanging in the tree above them. It didn't look to Simon like something that

should be hanging in a tree. It was like an obscene, giant child's mobile, except it appeared to be made from the bones of animals. It was clicking together slightly in the gentle wind, swaying from side to side. And as they looked, they saw that there was more than one such cluster. What they had earlier taken to be strange flowers were in fact three or four groups of hanging bones, fringing the tree in insane foliage. They stood and looked up at it in silence.

'I feel sick,' said Flora.

Simon did too, but he didn't say anything.

'Do you think they're . . . people's bones?' asked Flora.

And the thought immediately occurred to them both that they had been led there by the people on the bird-deer to see the final, frightful arrangement of their siblings' last remains. They instinctively moved closer to each other, but as they brushed together they almost immediately sprang apart.

'I know what you're thinking,' said Simon. 'But I don't think they're human. They're too small, for one thing.'

There was silence, except for the light breeze clicking the bones together. Simon imagined it

was the sound a giant might make gnashing and grinding his teeth, and, unbidden, a fragment of his childhood came back to him. His mother, leaning over him and his sister, whispering, '*Fee fi fo fum, I smell the blood of an Englishman.*'

Simon reached up.

'No!' said Flora.

Very lightly, he touched the nearest bunch of bones. His fingertip only grazed it, but it felt cool and hard.

He turned to Flora, indicating that he was about to pull the thing off the branch. 'Then we can examine it. It might tell us something,' he said, remembering the woman's message that help would come from places he didn't expect.

But Flora had her hand over her mouth.

Simon raised an eyebrow.

With her other hand, Flora pointed back to the tree.

Simon slowly turned round.

What had seemed to be bones were now not bones at all.

And they were moving.

They were unrolling into a thin sort of substance that looked like parchment, or leaves, or, thought

Simon with a sick lurch, skin. He felt it touch his hand and heard Flora scream. They were coming off the trees, crawling on to his body.

He watched in curious, astounded fascination as the things slid up his arm and unrolled and expanded. Now they were covering his whole torso.

He tried to pull one off, but it stuck. It hurt, as if he were attempting to rip off his own skin. He tried again, more frantically. It didn't work – if anything, it hurt more.

He looked towards Flora. She too was being wrapped up. Were these things alive?

Then Simon heard buzzing – high-pitched and awful. He saw Flora's face, looking at him, shocked out of all sense of normality. The things were creeping up towards his throat and he clawed at them, but they inched, inexorably, towards his face.

They're going over my mouth, he thought. His stomach heaved as he was quickly enveloped. He could not part his lips. His eyes were unpleasantly open. He could blink, but with great difficulty. He saw Flora as if through a layer of gauze. She'd fallen to the grass. He heaved himself towards her, though his legs were being bound together.

She was grappling with her new layer of skin. As

Simon struggled nearer Flora, he felt the substance tighten around his throat. An image came to him of his sister sitting in her room, holding a doll and murmuring to it. More memories: a dog barking, the smell of some laundry, a flower as tall as he was. Then he was unable to breathe and the world became dark.

He was nearing oblivion. *That's it*, he thought. *All over already. My sister gone. Myself gone. Nothing left.*

Then he felt the pressure lift a little. Simon found that he could gasp at the air. He scrabbled at his body. The extra skin was starting to come off without hurting him. It was sliding away of its own accord. Simon gulped down huge breaths, and sat upright, albeit with difficulty. He scrambled to his feet as quickly as he was able, and saw that Flora had also been released. She jumped up and ran to him. They stood, panting, watching what was happening.

The skin-like things were now crawling over the surface of the grass, undulating as if they were made of muscle. They moved towards each other, and joined into one shimmering whole.

'Are they . . . Is it . . . alive?' asked Flora.

Simon shrugged and coughed. 'Are you all right?'

'I think so . . . I don't know . . . Look!' said Flora.

The scrolls had settled now, and shrunk, and resembled nothing more than a large sheet of paper, or maybe parchment, Simon thought.

'There are markings on it . . .' said Flora. 'Let's go and see what —'

'No!' said Simon, but Flora had already run to it and knelt down. Simon held his breath, but nothing happened. It sat there, inanimate, as if it hadn't just leaped down from the trees and attacked them; as if their world had not been turned once more on its head.

'Come and see,' said Flora.

Simon inched towards it, then knelt beside her. Flora pointed to one side of it. 'There, look at the edge.'

Simon looked, and saw that on the right-hand edge, somewhere about the middle, there was a black circle with a line snaking towards it across the rest of the surface. Something about the black circle made him shiver.

Four letters were arranged in a cross at the top. By the black circle appeared what looked like a pair of horns.

'Devil's horns,' said Simon. He got up suddenly. He felt dizzy, ill. This was a sign, he knew it. They'd

been led there by the bird-deer people to find this thing, whatever it was, by the stone in the circle.

But he didn't want it. It felt wrong. Something about it made his stomach heave. He looked at Flora too, wondering whether he would have to travel with her all the way. All the way into that blackness.

That is where we're going, isn't it? he thought. The land of the Broken King. Into the darkness. Into the loneliness. It made him frightened.

'Look here as well,' said Flora, and pointed to the other edge. There was another circle, green this time. 'What is it?'

'How am I supposed to know?' said Simon shortly.

'What about these?' Flora pointed to the four letters. 'It looks a bit like writing. Sort of like *BENZ.*'

'*BENZ?* Like a Mercedes? Are you mad?' As Simon spoke the thing rolled itself up into a scroll, making them both jump. 'Look, are you coming or not? Let's go.' The clearing was too creepy to camp in. He wanted to find somewhere else.

'Where?'

'We'll find a field. I've got a tent.'

'But we can't –'

Simon had already picked up the scroll and started

off. So Flora, bemused, walked after him. She was glad to leave the circle too. *BENZ,* she thought. She wondered what it could mean. She paused for a second in the circle by the standing stone. For a moment, she thought she saw something white flashing in the forest to her left, but when she looked closer, it had gone.

Simon reached the edge of the clearing and looked ahead of himself at the darkening path. He turned back to see Flora standing uncertainly. Something inside him came loose and he was filled with pity. Whether he liked it or not, he supposed that this girl was going to be coming with him. 'Come on, Flora,' he called, as nicely as he was able. She flicked back her long black hair and smiled at him.

They set off, heading out of the woods. *And who knows what we'll find,* thought Simon as he strode ahead, the rucksack straps biting into his shoulders, and Flora half-running to catch up.

Chapter Four

Into
The Night

'WHAT DO WE do with it?'

Flora was lying on the grass outside the tent. They'd put it up with difficulty in the corner of a field about five minutes' walk from the circle with the stone. It was about eight o'clock in the evening. The sun was still up and the meadow was striped green and gold. Flora had stretched out the scroll and was staring at it. The letters – why were they arranged like that? In a cross. Almost like . . . like a compass. Then, suddenly, she slapped her forehead.

'Flora Williamson, you are an idiot!'

'What are you talking about?' said Simon, jolted from a reverie.

'I think it's a map,' said Flora. She pointed eagerly to the letters. '*BENZ!*'

'There you go again,' said Simon, putting his head back down on the cool grass.

'Oh, Simon!' exclaimed Flora, exasperated. 'Listen! B – E – N – Z. Why do you think they're arranged like they are?'

'Because some mad guy called Benz doodled his name on it. Because it's the property of a car dealership. I don't know. Whatever.'

Flora sighed and rolled her eyes. 'Directions! Look – *B*. Boreas. *E*. Eurus. *N* – I can't remember that one. And *Z* – Zephyrus!'

'Still none the wiser,' mumbled Simon.

'The winds, Simon! The winds!'

The light breeze ruffled her hair. Simon sat up suddenly and took the scroll. He scrutinised it carefully. 'So . . . it's like north, south, east and west. It's a map.'

'Of what, though?' said Flora, then, before Simon could reply added, 'Well, of where we have to go. It must be!'

'Well done, Flora!' Simon almost kissed her in

his exultation, but at the last minute turned his movement into an awkward hug.

Flora brushed him off. 'But it doesn't look like any map I've seen before. I mean, there's hardly anything on it. It's just a line and two circles and those letters. And . . .' She halted and blew the hair from her eyes. She couldn't quite put into words the slightly nauseous feeling she had about the map.

Simon leaned over it too. Every time he looked at the black circle on the right-hand side of it, he felt both exhilarated and fearful.

'What do you think those horns mean?' said Flora.

Simon thought a little. 'What has horns? Well, bulls, deer –'

'Like the bird-deer!'

'Yes . . . and also . . .' He looked at Flora's eyes. She was shading them from the sunlight. 'And also . . . devils.'

'Devils? But they don't . . . I mean, they don't exist . . .' Flora thought of red-skinned men with goat-feet holding forks and dancing about in cartoon flames.

They somehow didn't feel very frightening. Not as much as the blackness of that circle did, especially

when she stared at it too long.

'You've seen what you've seen and you're saying that they definitely don't exist? Why shouldn't they? I thought the woman on the deer was an angel . . . I asked her and she said . . . she said she was a messenger. Isn't that what an angel is? If they can exist, why not devils too?'

Flora tilted her head away from Simon. 'I suppose you're right. But they're not like any angel I've ever seen in books or films or anything.'

'That doesn't mean there won't be any devils, or something like devils. But it doesn't bring us any closer to knowing what this map is about.'

'Unless it's a map to . . .' She looked right back at Simon and lowered her eyes and her voice, and they both said at the same time, 'To hell.'

They spent the next couple of hours unmoving, stretched out on the ground. They talked from time to time about what the messengers might be. Could they really be angels? Not in the sense that they'd learned about in the Bible, that was for sure. But did it mean they were up against something dark, something terrible, that had taken their siblings? The Broken King . . . They tried to remember any scrap that they'd learned from children's rhymes,

but neither of them could recall anything apart from the rhyme for taking people away. Simon cursed, wishing he'd brought the book with him.

They'd pitched the tent behind a small clump of bushes, right at the edge of a field, away from the path. They heard and saw nobody walking along it, except for one walker whose dog, a black Labrador, came sniffing up to them, then turned away when a rabbit flashed by. It was so still they could hear the cars on the motorway beyond the hills. One honked its horn in the distance. The sun was lowering down and it was beginning to get cooler.

'You know I'm still not sure about this . . .' said Flora. 'We don't know where we're going, we've got no clues except this weird scroll thing . . . I just don't know what to do about it. Maybe I should just go home. Maybe Johnny doesn't want to be found.'

'I said it before,' said Simon, angry now, 'and I'll say it again. I'm going and I didn't ask you to come with me.'

'And I didn't ask to come!'

'Fine. Well, let's go to bed now, and in the morning we'll see. OK?'

Without looking at Flora, he crawled his way into the tent. They only had one sleeping bag, so he left

it for Flora and made a makeshift bed for himself out of the few clothes he'd brought with him.

After a while, Flora crawled in beside him. She seemed to consider the situation for a moment, and then unzipped the sleeping bag and cast it over both of them. They both lay awake, pretending to be asleep, for a long time. The tent grew warm with their breathing.

Flora couldn't sleep. After the tent became unbearably hot, she decided she'd sit outside in the cool darkness, and crawled out on her hands and knees, leaving Simon sleeping gently behind her.

Outside, she stretched. The moonlight was bright. What was it about the moon? It was almost full, hanging in the sky. She'd noticed it the night Johnny vanished.

She heard something move. *A rabbit*, she thought. She stiffened as the sound returned. No, something was coming towards her.

She couldn't understand what she was seeing. It seemed to to be a patch of greater darkness. Flora was looking at a slice of darkness. And it was moving. It filled her with fear. She wanted to run.

She saw it travelling towards the tent. It passed through a patch of moonlight. She saw fur and,

improbably, scales and teeth. Teeth that did not look as if they could possibly be in a mouth, since they were not near anything that might be a head.

Her first instinct was to flee. Then she thought of Simon – asleep, innocent, unknowing of the terror advancing. She was nearer the tent than the thing was. She started to sprint, as noiselessly as she could. She needed to warn Simon, find a weapon. But the creature was following. She could hear it snuffling.

She reached the tent flap and bent down to it. 'Wake up!' she whispered, then spoke louder. 'Wake up – quick!'

Muffled sounds came from inside. Flora sensed the creature behind her, turned, and before she could act it had leaped at her.

She felt its weight on her; it stank. She saw hot, bloody eyes and felt cool scales. Something tore at her; she screamed. She felt a light go on in the tent, heard the zip being undone. She beat off the beast, kicked it, stood up, saw it turn round to charge again, heard shouts from inside the tent.

A beam of light shone on the creature; Flora screamed. The creature changed tack and went for Simon, who'd just emerged.

Flora shouted again. Simon, who was still half asleep, was terrified at what he saw. There was Flora, hands held in front of her instinctively to protect herself. There was something – a blackness, a beast. He couldn't tell what it was but it was coming straight at him.

Simon flung his torch at the thing, then immediately wished he hadn't. The torch bounced off its hide and rolled away.

Then the creature was on him. It was about the size of a large dog, and he yelled as he felt its claws dig into him. Its stench choked his nostrils; its slobbering seemed to fill the world.

It's too strong, thought Simon, feeling it sniff along his body. *It's going to kill me. Before I've even left the county, I'm going to fail in my quest.*

A vast sadness filled him and he felt his body grow limp.

The creature, sensing its prey losing the will to live, readied itself to tear into his flesh.

I'm ready, thought Simon. *Ready.*

Then, as if from a huge distance, he heard another scream, but this time it sounded like encouragement.

Something was stabbing into the beast. It whined. It struggled and snapped.

'It won't get off him!'

That's Flora, thought Simon. Her voice made him remember. He had to get out of this. He stiffened his body, ready to try to push the thing off him.

He could feel someone slashing at the beast. Simon clamped his hands on its muzzle and stared into its burning eyes. They were hypnotic, terrible, evil. If he had been able to do so, he would have been sick at the smell coming off it. He was aware too of some scuffling around him.

'Help me!' he managed to yell.

Something tried to stab at the beast; the blow glanced off its scales. Again, and this time something cut into the flesh. The beast snarled.

'Get it off me!'

'I can't!' yelled Flora.

Simon gritted his teeth. He clamped down harder on the beast's muzzle with his right hand, and felt in his jeans pocket for something, pulling it out with difficulty. It was Anna's porcupine spine.

'Simon!' shouted Flora. 'Look out!'

Another stab of a knife just missed his shoulder. Simon tensed himself and thrust as hard as he could with the spine, right into the creature's eye. It snarled and whimpered. He felt it relax. He jabbed the spine

deep into the cavity of its other eye, and he felt its body go limp. He threw it off, and then someone else was beside him, sticking a knife again and again into its body. The whole thing shivered and convulsed; two spurts of blood shot out from where an artery must have been hit, and then it was still.

Simon collapsed on to the ground, and was immediately and violently sick. Over his retching he heard Flora shouting, 'Hey, come back!'

Flora was panting. The shock of what she'd seen came over her suddenly, but she steadied herself. She was bleeding. A boy had come out of the woods with a knife – she ran towards the edge of the trees and looked for him, but couldn't see anything. He'd run off. If he hadn't come . . . She hadn't been able to see much of him. Who was he? A noise from Simon made her turn back to him.

Simon was bent over, wiping his mouth. Flora went tenderly to his side.

'Are you all right?' Her voice sounded loud in the quiet. An owl hooted and a bat dived across them into the woods.

Simon stopped retching. He was breathing deeply, heavily. 'I think so,' he said. He felt a dull pain all over his body.

'Here.' Flora rushed into the tent and came out with some water, which she gave to Simon. He drank it in one go. When he'd finished, she asked, 'Did you see him?'

Simon was now lying on his back, clutching the spine he'd stabbed the creature with. He released his grip, slowly. He wiped the spine on the grass, cleansing it of blood, and placed it back in his pocket.

'See who?'

'The boy. The other boy. He came and stabbed that thing with a knife.'

'No,' said Simon. 'I had other things to worry about.' He smiled ruefully.

'Glad to see you're feeling OK,' said Flora.

'Who was he, then?' *So there had been someone else*, thought Simon. A boy – a boy with a knife. Was he following them? If he was an enemy, why had he saved them? Was he an emissary of the Broken King? The Knight of the Swan? Was he one of the Golden People? There had been no light around him, though.

'I didn't get a chance to look at him properly. He was a boy. I didn't really see his face. He looked . . .' Flora stopped herself. 'He looked . . . well, like he didn't have a home to go to.' She remembered grey,

loose clothes, and a pale, pudgy face with eyes that gleamed.

'He helped us,' said Simon. 'We should find him – thank him. We could have died.'

'Let's get you cleaned up first. I didn't see where he went, and he could be anywhere by now.' She placed the torch between two stones, so that it cast its beam upon Simon's face. He was sweating and pale. Flora got out another bottle of water and washed him down gently. The small bite on his shoulder was only skin deep, and the claw marks were superficial. Simon looked at Flora's wound and put some antiseptic on it.

'What do you think it was?' said Simon, wheezing.

'I don't know. Some kind of dog. But a weird kind of dog . . .' Flora took the torch and said, 'Are you ready to look at it?'

Simon nodded.

She shone the torch on to where the creature had fallen.

There was nothing there except a small area of brown grass. Remembering their conversation about devils, she shuddered and moved the torch back to Simon.

'Do you think it's run off? Do you think it will

come back? Maybe we should move on . . .' said Simon, his voice quavering a little.

'I don't know,' said Flora. 'It looked pretty dead to me after you stabbed it, and that boy finished it off . . . He ran off afterwards.'

'But do you think there'll be more of them?' *These are the dangers the golden woman warned about*, he thought. He suddenly felt angry. They'd been thrown into this journey with nothing – no guide, no help. Nothing apart from the porcupine spine, and that had come from Anna.

'Right,' said Simon. 'You sleep and I'll watch.'

'Fine. Wake me up at four and I'll take over.'

'Don't worry about it. I don't think I can sleep anyway.'

'Wake me up if you hear anything.' She paused. 'You should have something you can use as a weapon. Other than the spine, I mean.'

They cast around outside the tent as far as they dared, keeping very close together and sweeping the torchbeam around the ground, to find a couple of large sticks.

So Flora went to bed, straight into a dreamless sleep.

Simon wrapped himself up in several layers of

clothes, though he didn't really need them – they were more for comfort than anything else. He held on to one stick, and kept the other behind him. *Just in case*, he thought. The night sky was clear. He tried to remember what he could of constellations, but could only recognise the saucepan-shape of the Great Bear.

What had that thing been? Some kind of bear? Maybe it was something that had escaped from a zoo – there was one nearby, wasn't there? Perhaps a panther? He'd read about animals escaping from private menageries too.

Or maybe it was something else, something that came from that black hole on the map, that place where he knew they had to go. Those horns . . . devil horns . . . Were they really going into hell? He unrolled the map scroll, and stared at it for a long time, thinking, alert to every sound.

Chapter Five

EAT THE SHADOW, STEAL THE SUN, BREAK THE AIR

S IMON FELT IT first: the warmth of the sun as it came over the tops of the trees. The dawn light was clear and precise, each leaf of each tree cut sharply from the air. He'd not slept at all, partly through fear and partly because of the adrenaline rushing through his veins. He was intrigued, too, by the boy who'd suddenly appeared to help them fight the creature and wanted to see if he would come back. There'd been no sign of him, though.

As the sun grew higher, he recognised a deeper warmth. Joy entered his heart, and he knew what had come. He turned and there in the clearing were

the two messengers seated on their winged mounts, their faces grave and sculpted. One man, one woman. The bird-deer stood still, as if they knew that they had to be silent.

Flora felt it too and crawled out of the tent. The sickness and the horror of the night vanished, dispelled.

The messengers spoke, both at the same time, though as before, it was not really as if words had been said at all.

'We came when we could. Show it to us.'

Simon, knowing immediately what they meant, pulled out the scroll. 'What is it?' he asked, laying it in front of them. His face was prickling with sweat.

'It will show you the way. It was difficult to get. But be thankful for it.'

'Where will the map take us?' asked Flora, scratching her chin.

'First it must be activated. It will show you the way to the three Hidden Things, each in turn, and then to where your siblings are kept in the halls of the Broken King. It will be harder than we'd thought. You are known, but we did not expect that attack last night. You did well.'

'Known to who?' said Flora. 'The Broken King?'

'To him, yes, and to his helpers. Simon has seen the Knight of the Swan already, though they are not all like that.'

'The creature . . . last night? The swan, before? They're all helpers of the Broken King?'

'The creature was one of the royal hounds. They will try to stop you.'

'Tell us more,' said Simon.

Everything went dark. And then Simon and Flora found themselves looking into somewhere else. They saw something that looked like a cliff, black and menacing, and something like a skyscraper on top of it, each window lit with silver light. And they saw shadows swarming and moving around it.

There were many more tall glass buildings, black and featureless, and there were long, straight black roads full of people, all rushing by with their heads down. Carts lumbered along, pulled by beasts that looked like horses but didn't seem quite right. A man in black armour fitted closely to his body stalked along the road, and all made a path for him. Music issued from the buildings, discordant and fast, and trees twisted their branches up into the dark sky where a large crescent moon hung low. Simon saw the same bone shapes they'd seen in the clearing

hanging on the trees, and he shuddered.

Now Simon was in a room, echoey and large, and he could see Anna standing in the corner of it. Could he speak to her? He ran to her, but she was staring listlessly into the distance and he found that he couldn't even touch her.

There was someone else with her, a boy, but he couldn't see him properly. His face was turned away. Simon turned closer to Anna. There was something horribly wrong with her, something that was making him want to cry out, but he couldn't make a sound.

The vision vanished, leaving Simon and Flora gasping.

'The Broken King has put up barriers and made it impossible for us to go to them. There is one way, though, for you. There is a story in your world, where a hero has to pluck a golden bough from a tree to visit the underworld. He likes that story, but thinks it's too easy. And so he has set three tasks. If you complete them all, then you can enter the kingdom.'

'Why has he taken our siblings?'

Flora's voice sounded clear and bright. Simon was a little startled.

If it was possible for the messengers' expressions to change, they did. The female bowed her head, and

the male shook his. They did not answer at first.

'You called him,' they said.

'There must be more to it than that,' said Flora.

The messengers said nothing.

'Is it the . . . underworld?' said Simon. 'Is it . . . Hell?'

'No,' replied the messengers. 'It has many names, but there is nowhere like what you speak of.'

'But it's not in our world,' said Simon.

'We exist in your universe, on the same plane. So do they. There are walls between us, though. That is why we appear like we do. We are like . . . projections, made out of the light of the sun. They use the shadows, and can control some of the beasts in your world.'

'What should we do?' said Flora.

'To gain entry to the Broken Kingdom you must do three things. Eat the shadow.'

It was as before: a vision, or a way into another version of reality, but whatever it was Simon and Flora saw themselves standing in front of their tent, as if they were looking down from above, and then their bodily selves vanished.

They had been cloaked somehow, invisible to the world.

'Steal the sun.'

The image before them changed to something out of a dream Simon had had before, of a great arc of fire leaping out of a boiling mass, and it formed into a bright shard, which Simon reached out to take but vanished before his hand.

'Break the air.'

The world was full of noise; Simon's ears rang and the ground shook as if they were in the throes of a small earthquake. He felt a force that could tear buildings to the ground. He'd forgotten Flora, but he turned to her now. He saw her standing, face white, eyes wide. She stumbled; he held out a hand for her to grab but she didn't take it.

The visions came to an end. Simon and Flora stood sweating. A plane overhead left a silver line in the sky. Simon wondered whether he could hear it, or whether the buzzing was just in his mind. The golden messengers stared down at them. The man's bird-deer pawed the ground and snorted.

'Are our siblings alive?' said Simon. He thought of Anna in that dark place.

'Yes,' said the woman.

'Can't you . . . can't you come? Do we have to go there alone?'

Both bird-deer shrank back, their nostrils

quivering. They stamped their little hooves and their wingtips twitched, though the man and the woman, as ever, stayed expressionless as flint.

'We cannot go. It would be war. It is close enough already. You must start now. They will only attack at night, but they have agents in the daytime also. Be wary. There will be some who will help you and some who will hinder you. Look for birds, fire, gold. Trapped inside the first place are those who will aid you, if you free them.'

The golden messengers stroked their mounts and wheeled them round.

'Wait!' said Simon, strength returning to him. 'How do we know where to go? What does it mean? Eat the sun . . . steal the shadow . . . I don't understand!'

They turned their mounts away, throwing no shadows upon the earth. The bird-deer put their heads forward, stretching their necks. The two golden messengers leaned down, and the bird-deer started lifting up their feet, first at a run and then at a gallop. They arced in a wide circle around the two friends and then took off, soaring into the blueness of the sky, leaving Flora and Simon staring after them half blinded.

Simon sat down in the grass, his hair plastered to his forehead. 'I don't understand,' he said again plaintively to Flora, who was still standing with her arms folded, looking as if she'd just been through a whirlwind. She paced round in a circle, and the movement reminded Simon even more forcibly of when he'd last seen Anna. He put his arm over his eyes and choked back a sob. In the vision, she'd been in some sort of prison, and something about her had been wrong, so wrong that even as he thought of it he shuddered. 'I don't . . .' he said again, defeated, and he let his arm lie over his eyes.

'I do,' said Flora.

Simon ignored her.

'Look, you,' said Flora, coming towards him. She still had her arms folded and her eyes were screwed up in concentration.

'What do you know, anyway?' said Simon, feeling uncomfortable. He lowered his arm and saw Flora standing over him.

'I know. What this is.' She held the scroll out to him. 'It's them, Simon.'

'What are you talking about?'

'It's them!' she said again. 'It's how we're going to find them. It's them.'

'What's wrong with you? What's the matter? You're crying . . .'

'Can't you see? Didn't you see what they were like?' Flora said desperately.

Simon remembered. Anna and the figure beside her in that dark, vast room. He remembered how he couldn't look at her properly. He remembered now what was wrong with her. She'd stretched out her arms towards him – although of course she hadn't seen him, how could she? – and what he had seen made him recoil.

They were hands, all right. But they didn't have any skin.

'Oh my God,' he said.

'It's them, Simon,' said Flora again. 'It's their skin . . . I saw Johnny, Simon. I saw Johnny . . . and his face, Simon. Half of his face was gone.'

Chapter Six

SUPERMARKET
SWEEP

FLORA AND SIMON packed up their tent. The skin-map, flayed from the living bodies of their siblings, lay to one side.

'In books,' said Simon, as he rolled up the tent into a tight bundle, 'messengers are always enigmatic. You'd have thought that when you actually came across one in actual real life that it would, you know, tell you where to go directly instead of being all poetic and weird about it . . .' He was covering up his agitation. He knew very well – or at least thought he knew well – why the messengers' instructions were obscure. It was part of his punishment.

He looked at Flora and wondered what her brother had done to her to make her say the rhyme. She caught his hard gaze and glared back at him from under her eyelashes.

When they'd packed everything up, they sat down and looked at the skin-map. Both of them were shaking inwardly at the image they'd seen of their siblings. Simon thought of Anna's outstretched hands; Flora could not stop thinking about her brother's face – his kind, confused, mutilated face . . . Would he ever be the same again? Suddenly it was too much for her and she let her tears flow. Simon laid a hand on her shoulder.

She sniffed and brushed it off. 'It's OK. There must be a reason for it. It's their skin, so perhaps it's so we can find them. It will lead us to them. Maybe it didn't hurt. They're trapped and it's a way for us to get to them.'

'Let's hope so,' said Simon quietly. He felt a hollowness inside. He wondered if Anna had made a sacrifice for him, if she'd known that her skin would be used, if she'd even volunteered it.

Still, neither of them wanted to touch the map until Simon said, 'OK. Let's think of it like this: if we pick it up, it'll be like we've got them with us.

It's obviously meant to take us to them. So it's like having a . . . forerunner to guide us.'

Flora crumpled up her face and then nodded. 'OK, then. You go first.'

Simon imagined that he was reaching out to hold Anna's hand, and the thought comforted him. When he held the map, it felt warm and alive, but this did not trouble him. It was Anna – or part of her. He unrolled it. There was the blackness at the far side and the curious sign of the pair of horns.

'So this is where we have to go,' he said. 'But there are no markings to guide us – well, no normal markings.'

'No petrol stations,' said Flora. 'Or good intentions.' She smiled at Simon.

'What?'

'They do say the road to hell is paved with good intentions.'

'What?'

'Nothing. I was just thinking out loud.'

'I suppose our only option,' said Simon, batting away a fly, 'is really to head here . . . but in which direction is it? I mean, if it's like a normal map, then that would be just slightly west of north. The winds tell us that. But how do we even know it's a map

of here? It could be anywhere. It could be Japan. It could be the moon . . .'

'And we've got to do those three things the messengers told us to do before we can get there.'

'Eat the shadow,' said Simon.

'Steal the sun.'

'Break the air.'

In the pause Simon thoughtfully played with the porcupine spine in his pocket. He drew it out and flicked it over and over. It had served him once before. There were the button and the pencil stub too. He took the three objects and placed them on the grass. *You will find help in unexpected places*, he thought.

Flora stood up. The sun was behind her. Her hair played around her face and she brushed it away from her eyes. There was a trail of tears glistening on her cheek.

Simon stretched and knelt in front of the map. He took the pencil and wrote his name on it.

'They said it had to be activated. We have to do something to it. What could it be?' asked Simon. He heard a noise – a blackbird fluttering away. He remembered the boy who'd saved them. *Maybe he's watching*, thought Simon, and he looked around . . . but he saw nothing.

'Let's think about it logically,' said Flora. She liked the sound of the word. 'What are you doing, by the way?'

Simon had put the button on the map. He shrugged. 'Just playing around.' He took it off again and slipped it back into his pocket, noting its greenness as it went in.

'This has come from our siblings. It was taken from them so that we can find them. So maybe we have to give it something of our own?'

'How do you mean? Do you mean cut off our own skin?' Simon asked, his face incredulous.

'No, I don't. I mean . . . what if it needs to be something from us. Like – like our blood.'

The world was still for a moment as Simon thought about this. 'Well, Anna gave me something once. It was the only thing she'd ever given me, actually.' He took the porcupine up from the grass. 'I used it to stab that . . . creature in the eye. I could use it to . . .'

'To prick yourself?' said Flora quietly.

Simon found the first aid kit. There was a little bottle of antiseptic in it. He unscrewed the lid and dipped the spine into it, then washed it off with a splash of water. 'That thing must have had some

pretty nasty diseases,' he said, smiling a little. 'Right. Here goes, I guess.' Simon took the porcupine spine and carefully pricked the end of his finger. He watched a tiny drop of blood form on the end of it. It fell on to the map.

'Now what?'

'I hadn't thought about that.'

'Well, we need to tell it what to do,' said Flora.

Using the spine, Simon formed the words *EAT THE SHADOW* in his blood, and waited.

'Look, Flora!'

They both saw that the map was becoming more detailed. Here was a copse, there a road leading out of it. It started to take on the familiar contours of the county they were in.

'Well, that's a relief,' said Flora. 'At least it's not Japan.'

'Look, I recognise this. There's Limerton on the coast. That's the road to Moreton-on-the-Green. And this road, the one we want, leads further north to . . .'

'Sainsbury's?' said Flora, recognising where the black circle now was, by a roundabout.

'Well,' said Simon. 'Whoever thought that the mouth to hell would be under the frozen goods aisle?'

'Well then,' said Flora. 'There's only one thing for it.'

'To the supermarket!' said Simon.

And laughing, though grimly, the two of them set off. Simon rolled up the map and put it in his pocket alongside the porcupine spine.

'We should try to work out what they mean, shouldn't we?' said Simon. 'I mean, the tasks.'

'I was thinking that too,' replied Flora, looking back over her shoulder at him. They were walking beneath some telephone lines, and she'd been thinking about all the voices travelling along them, meeting, loving, hating.

'Think about the visions we saw. In the first one, about the shadow, something happened to us and we couldn't see ourselves. I think that's easy,' said Simon.

'What do you mean?'

'A shadow cloaks, doesn't it? So whatever it is, it's something that will cloak us, disguise us. They said we wouldn't be able to go there – to the Broken Kingdom – as we are, didn't they?'

'You're right. So *eat the shadow* means a disguise,' said Flora. 'How about *steal the sun?*'

'That one's pretty easy too. Think about the demon creature. The messengers said there'd be more. In

the vision I had there was a weapon or something, so I think it's that – a sword or something that can kill those creatures.'

'OK. How about the third? Break the air?'

Simon remembered the noise, like the world shaking. It was uncomfortably like the noise that had happened when he'd said the rhyme and Anna had been taken. He shrugged. 'I don't know,' he said. 'It's got me stumped.'

'It reminded me of something, though,' said Flora.

'When . . . when your brother was taken?'

Flora ignored him. 'Something I learned at school, something about . . . walls tumbling down. I'll get it in a minute . . .'

But she didn't.

'What do those instructions actually mean, though? I mean, surely they don't mean we actually have to *eat* the shadow, do we? How can you eat a shadow? A shadow is nothing, isn't it?'

'A shadow is still something. Think about *Peter Pan*. It's like a shadow is a bit of yourself.'

'You mean we'll have to eat a bit of ourselves? That would be . . . gross!'

A thought struck both of them, uneasily, at the same time.

'The map . . .'

'No,' said Simon with emphasis. 'It absolutely can't mean that. Without the map we wouldn't know where to go.'

'So what do you think we should do?'

'I think we should just go to the supermarket.'

'Right,' said Flora, though she didn't sound convinced.

It wasn't far to the supermarket. Flora and Simon decided to follow a minor road alongside which there was a track screened by trees, so it was hard to be seen by anyone driving along. Flora cleaned herself up in a stream and Simon put on a fresh T-shirt – a multi-coloured stripy one – and both were feeling better. They had a destination. Simon was picturing Anna sitting amongst the chocolates in the supermarket aisle, like when they'd last gone there and she hadn't wanted to leave.

A Range Rover went past, a dog hanging mournfully out of its window. Sometimes a truck with piles of wood in the back, or a car, would dash by, and no one slowed down at the sight of two teenagers out for a walk on a summer morning.

Flora started to hum as they walked, and then broke out into song. It was a hymn that Simon

recognised, 'Jerusalem', and Simon joined in, quietly at first, but when they reached the bit about *dark Satanic mills*, he positively belted it out, and laughing trotted after Flora.

As he did, a little red car, nothing very special, did a U-turn as it went past them.

Flora and Simon soon stood at the edge of a road. The green-edged path came to an end; in front of them was the concrete hulk of the roundabout, with its bold, bare signs and some marigolds that the municipal council obviously thought decorative. Here the road widened and met three others, busier by far, that shot vehicles into view like bullets. The pair hovered uncertainly, like rabbits.

'Now what?'

'Well, I wasn't expecting a sign,' said Flora.

'*Abandon hope, all ye who enter here?*'

'That's wrong. It's *abandon all hope, ye who enter here,*' said Flora,

'That's really helpful.'

The car that had done a U-turn came around the roundabout and entered the supermarket car park. Flora saw a young man with black hair and blue eyes was driving it, a lit cigarette in his mouth that he then ashed out of the window. Flora shook her

head. 'Bad habit,' she said. She turned to Simon.

"Well, no,' said Simon. 'First, what shall we do until then? And second, think about it. *Eat the shadow.* There aren't really any shadows around at night, are there?'

'That's 'cause everything is in shadow. But we can't go around in broad daylight. What if we get recognised?'

'We don't know what's going to happen down there. It could be worse than that . . . demon thing. If anything, you can't go on your own. You might need me.'

'I don't think those devil things can come out in the day. Isn't that what the messengers said?'

'Yes, but even so . . . Look.' Simon shifted the rucksack off his shoulder, unzipped it and rummaged around until he found what he was looking for. 'Here.' He put on a pair of sunglasses that had been left there from a previous trip and stretched out both his hands, making an actorly kind of face. 'I don't want to be recognised.'

'All right then, big shot,' said Flora. 'Let's go.'

'No photos!' said Simon, and Flora, despite herself, laughed.

They made a plan: Simon would look round

the inside of the supermarket. Flora would search around the outside. 'It's easier for me to explain myself,' she said. 'Girls can get away with stuff easier than boys. If someone asks me what I'm doing I'll just look lost, mumble something, and then make a sharp exit. Oh,' she said, as they came to the entrance of the car park. 'What are we looking for anyway?'

Simon shrugged. 'I think we'll know it when we see it.' He held out his hand. Flora took it and shook it sharply, then made a salute. 'See you, soldier,' she said, and skipped off. 'Back here in half an hour at the latest, whatever happens, OK?'

'OK!' said Simon, giving her a half grin, half grimace.

Trying to look as inconspicuous as possible, Simon walked down towards the supermarket. He saw a woman wearing a padded jacket slam the door of her car and two of her children get out, and recognised them as living in Limerton, near his house, and sped up.

The supermarket, ugly and red brick, rose monstrously in front of him. People spewed out as yet more flowed into it. They dragged with them trolleys bulging with piles of plastic bags full of food. He slipped in through the automatic

doors where a uniformed guard stood, and into the anaemic, cold atmosphere inside.

He stopped dead in his tracks. His neighbour, Francis Weston, was rooting amongst the vegetables, picking up aubergines and eyeing them critically. *Oh no*, Simon thought, and edged behind a flower stall.

Outside, Flora stood on the tarmac, feeling the heat rising. The supermarket was built out of red brick and glass; a cavernous building that loomed out of the fields.

Eat the shadow, steal the sun, break the air. We have to do all those things, she thought, *before we can enter that place, where that creature came from, and where they've got Johnny.* An immediate, fierce need to see her brother again enveloped her.

As she rounded the corner of the building, she remembered the last time she'd seen him. He'd been having one of his good phases.

It was breakfast. He was thin and pale, wearing a band T-shirt and the leather jacket he never took off. He'd been smoking a roll-up.

'That's disgusting,' said Flora, taking it off him. She stubbed it out in the sink and looked at Johnny reproachfully.

'At least leave me one thing, Flors,' he said.

She sat down on the kitchen table and cried.

'Why are you crying?'

It all flooded out. 'You're the favourite child. Everyone loves you. Everyone dances around you, even though you're a drop out. You dropped out of Cambridge, you've been arrested I don't know how many times, you get in trouble with the police, and you can still do nothing wrong. Whenever you come home it's just Johnny this and Johnny that and nobody ever talks about me or thinks about me. I've got my exams coming up this year and no one's even asked me what I'm studying . . . I want to go to Cambridge too and I won't drop out . . . and now Mum and Dad are . . . divorcing . . . I feel . . . broken.'

He took his jacket off and put it round her shivering shoulders, and then, without saying anything, he went upstairs. Looking for a tissue, she put her hands in his pockets, and that was when she found the syringe.

The anger overwhelmed her. She ran upstairs, past the piles of laundry in various states, past her mother's open bedroom door through which she could see her mother on the bed watching television, on up to her room.

Sulking there, she found an old book they'd read as little children together called *In the Land of the Broken King*. She flicked through its pages, tears prickling at her eyes, until she reached the poem.

Spitefully, she'd stomped around the room, wishing and wishing that Johnny would be taken, that she could be on her own, that people would listen to her and not to him, that the whole problem of his life would be gone.

Next morning, she remembered little except the rhyme. She ran into the attic room where Johnny had his den and burst through the door.

There was the poster of Bob Marley. There was the pool table with a cue lying alongside it. There were the crushed beer cans, and the wine bottles used as candle holders that he thought were really cool. His bed, unmade, with its Union Jack duvet that he'd had for as long as Flora could remember. The window open, the stale smell of smoke. The philosophy books, half-read.

But no Johnny.

They had searched all day, all around the house, then in the nearby towns, in the bars that he used to hang out in. His friends hadn't seen him. His girlfriend hadn't heard from him. The police . . . The

police were not interested in a boy over eighteen.

That night Flora had sat awake, watching the moon, oblivious of everything but its cold light. She knew there was no point in searching; that she'd wished him gone. And, though she hadn't seen it, that something had heard her say the rhyme, and taken him.

The next morning the messenger came.

A tear fell down her cheek.

'It's too lovely a day to be crying,' said a voice.

Flora came back sharply to reality and saw an old lady standing by the overflowing bins.

'I wasn't crying', said Flora, wiping away the tear.

'That looked like a tear to me,' said the old lady.

She was quite tall for an old lady, thought Flora. She was wearing a thick grey cardigan, a long brown skirt and very sensible-looking brown shoes. She held herself rather upright.

'Trouble with your boyfriend?' asked the old lady. 'You can call me Auntie, if you like.'

Flora, wary, shook her head. 'I'm looking for something,' she said.

The old lady smiled. 'Aren't we all?' she said. 'Aren't we all, my dear? Maybe – depending on what sort of thing it is – I can help you find it.'

Maybe she's here to help us, thought Flora, and reached for her phone – then remembered she didn't have it, and couldn't call Simon.

'Maybe you can,' she said.

Simon was avoiding Francis Weston in the crisps aisle when he decided to look at the map. He unrolled it and, hiding behind a stack of huge bags on offer, studied it.

The black circle was pulsing. *We must be near*, thought Simon. He'd just rolled it up again and put it back in his pocket when someone tapped him on the shoulder. *Oh no*, thought Simon. *Francis Weston.*

He turned round and instead of his neighbour saw a wild-looking boy in a tracksuit who was hopping from leg to leg and breathing heavily.

'Simon!' The boy also seemed to know his name. 'Simon, you gotta come now! Flora, she's outside with some old lady . . .'

It might be a trap, thought Simon. 'How do I know you're telling the truth?'

The boy looked exasperated. 'It was me – me who saved you. Come on!' He turned and walked off quickly.

Simon went after him. 'Saved me from what?'

'That thing . . . Look!' He pulled up his T-shirt and showed Simon the scar that the creature had made. It was revolting, weeping slightly round the edges, and Simon gagged.

'Oh Jesus . . . That's horrible . . .' Simon's revulsion turned to gratitude. He remembered the stink of the creature, and how close he'd come to death.

'But . . . how . . . can I thank you?' His mind whirled. He looked at the boy. He was about the same age as him, and was a little podgy, with black hair and very pale skin. He looked agitated.

'Have you been following us?' said Simon.

The boy hesitated.

'You have been following us! Why?'

The boy looked confused. 'I . . .'

'How can I trust you?'

'Just come!'

'What's your –'

'Pike,' said Pike, and set off.

Simon, thinking that following him would at least take him somewhere, went after him.

They came outside to see Flora standing by the bins with an old lady. Simon was about to join her when Pike pulled him back and whispered, 'No. There's something weird about her.'

'Flora?'

Pike rolled his eyes. 'The old lady. Her hands. Her teeth. Her hair.' Pike couldn't explain it, but he knew it. He could feel it, somewhere deep in his bones.

Concealed behind some bins, they waited and listened to the conversation. Cars roared past on the road beside them.

'What's your name, my dear?' said the old lady. 'Would you like a sweet?' She rummaged around in a large handbag which hung on her arm and pulled out a paper bag full of big, brown, chewy-looking lumps. She proffered them, smiling and revealing her brownish teeth to Flora.

'Flor . . . ence,' said Flora. 'And . . . no, thank you.'

'Girls these days,' said the old lady. 'Always worrying about how they look.'

'No, it's not that,' said Flora, irked a little. 'I just –'

'So what are you looking for?' said the old lady. 'Love?'

Yuck, thought Simon.

'No,' said Flora, flustered. 'I'm looking for something that will help me find my brother.'

'And who's your brother?'

That's a strange question, thought Flora. 'He's –

well . . . Why are you so interested anyway?'

The old lady laughed and put her hands up, clapping them together. 'Just curious. Just want to help a little lady like yourself.' She reached out and placed a hand on Flora's shoulder. Flora could smell talcum powder and dog. It reminded Flora of her own grandmother.

'Are you sure you don't want a sweet?' said the old lady gently.

Why shouldn't I take one? thought Flora dreamily. She's only an old lady.

The old woman's grip was soft on her shoulder, caressing her, reminding her that someone else could take charge, that somebody else could look after her.

Maybe I will have that sweet, thought Flora. The old lady reached into her handbag with her other hand, and pulled out one of the delicious-looking fudges. She held it in front of Flora's face. Her grip on Flora's shoulder tightened, almost imperceptibly. The fingers were strangely hard.

'Hey,' said Flora, some signal reaching through to her brain.

'What is it, my dear?'

'You're . . . hurting me,' said Flora. She reached

up and tried to prise the old lady's hand off her. But she couldn't. 'What are you doing?'

'Well, dear, it wouldn't do, would it, to let you in.'

'What do you mean?'

'The king would not be happy . . .' The old lady's smile grew wider, and as it did, her teeth elongated and her skin tightened up and her body stretched. 'I've been guarding this place, so carefully, for so long . . .'

The pain in Flora's shoulder was awful, from the strong fingers of the old lady – although she wasn't so much of an old lady now, she was . . . *What* is *she?* thought Flora. She heard the shouts of supermarket workers near by going about their business and the overwhelming sounds of a lorry reversing preceded its back poking round the corner.

'There are doors within doors and worlds within worlds,' said the old lady. 'My role is an important one. Nobody can get in. Nobody. The king would not be happy. You want to set them free, do you? It is not going to happen. You want the shadow? I will not let you have it. Behind me is the door, but no one can go through. Nobody has gone through since the last ones – and they are trapped.'

Flora tried to scream but the creature now had its hand over her mouth. Heat shimmered off the tarmac around them.

'We've got to help her!' whispered Simon urgently.

Pike nodded, and they leaped out from behind the bins, causing a cardboard box perched on the top to fall on to the ground amongst the wrapped lettuces and flapping newspapers.

The creature swung round at the noise, maintaining its grip on Flora who tried unsuccessfully to prise the hand off her shoulder.

The thing was tall now, with brownish, shrunken skin and long teeth. It was still wearing its old woman clothes as Flora kicked and squealed.

'And what are you?' it said, looking at Simon and Pike, its voice hissing and cold.

'Let her go,' said Simon, more bravely than he thought he could.

Pike hurled a stone at the creature's head. It glanced off the side, but threw it off enough to loosen its grip. Flora broke free and scampered over to where the two of them stood. Pike was jumping from foot to foot; he felt alive and his nostrils were dilating.

'The boy!' said Flora. 'The one who rescued us!'

'His name's Pike,' said Simon.

'No time for introductions,' said Flora, and pointed at the thing.

The creature bent down and lifted something up.

Simon gaped. The creature had picked up the shadow of the bin, and was now unrolling it like a ream of cloth, spreading it out and holding it up between its hands where it hung, almost opaque. It shifted the shadow round and round as if it were a sheet of shimmering black silk.

'Quick,' said Pike, picking up another stone and throwing it. The creature was advancing towards them with the shadow.

'Look behind it!' said Flora. There was a loading bay behind the creature, and inside it she could see something. 'It looks like a door. Quick, Simon, the map!'

Nothing else for it, thought Pike. He ran towards the creature and launched himself at it, knocking it down to the ground. The creature dropped the shadow, which slid back to its accustomed place.

Flora ran at it too and sat on its arms while Pike held on to its legs. The creature writhed and snapped. A plastic bag floated past them.

Scrabbling, Simon unrolled the map. There was the black dot, and it was pulsing faster now.

'This must be it,' he said. He looked up into the loading bay. There, just inside the entrance, was a shape in the air. It wasn't so much definitely a door as the impression of a door. He went up to it and felt all round it, then pushed at it. It resisted.

'Hurry, Simon!' shouted Flora.

'I don't know how to open it!' he said.

Pike was looking around, trying to work out how to put the creature out of action. He thought about the knife that he kept in his pocket, but somehow that revolted him. This wasn't a beast like that other creature . . . He looked into its eyes and saw intelligence looking back at him. For a second he almost relaxed, but then renewed his efforts when he felt the creature tensing and gathering its strength.

'Ouch!' It was Flora. The creature had kneed her in the side. 'Simon!'

Simon looked back at them, struggling on the ground. *Oh Lord*, he thought. He felt around the door one more time, looking for a gap, for anything that might be of use. All he could find was a small, roundish dip in one edge.

Then he remembered the button. *The help*, he thought. *They left it for us, they must have done.* He fished it out quickly.

Pike meanwhile had noticed a long metal pole by the side of the bins. If only he could reach it, then they could knock the creature out. 'Flora!' he shouted.

How does this boy know my name? thought Flora, and reasoned that Simon must have told him. Pike nodded towards the pole and Flora realised what he wanted her to do.

'On the count of three,' he whispered.

He nodded once.

Simon held the button out.

The creature lashed and bucked underneath Pike.

Simon fitted the button into the dip, holding his breath. *I must be crazy,* he thought. He heard Pike yell out. *Come on,* he thought. The button clicked into place with a satisfying sound. Something shifted; he pushed against the outline of the door.

Pike nodded for the third time and Flora leaped across to where the pole was lying. The creature rose up and grabbed Pike by the arms before hurling him down. Flora threw the pole to Pike. It fell beside him; he picked it up and swung it round, just hitting the creature on the head as it reached towards him. It swayed and shook.

Simon pressed forwards. 'The door!' he shouted. 'It's opening!'

The creature fell to its knees. Pike got up, took a bigger swing, knocked it round the side of the head and, almost like a tree, it toppled. He whacked it again, harder, and it fell to the tarmac. Pike stood there, panting.

'Into the door!' shouted Simon. He looked through. He could see nothing inside except blackness and he felt a terrible fear, a sickness. *I must overcome it*, he thought. *I must.*

Simon squared his shoulders. 'In I go, then,' he said, and Flora followed. Pike, whose mind had become a roiling mass of alarm, went through after her.

And as Pike's back disappeared into the blackness, a young man came around the corner of the building. If Simon had seen him, he'd have recognised him as the swan who'd turned into a man, who the woman on the bird-deer had called Sir Mark, the Knight of the Swan.

He'd parked his little red car up by the supermarket and had been watching with interest all the time. He looked at the creature lying on the tarmac and kicked it dismissively.

'Rubbish,' he drawled. He yawned and ran his fingers through his black hair. 'Can't anyone do their job properly any more?'

He brought his fingers together in front of him and flexed his muscles. He opened his mouth and a strange, unearthly sound came out of it. He circled the thing on the tarmac once, anti-clockwise.

The thing stirred, opened its eyes and saw the Knight of the Swan.

'Sir Mark . . .'

'You have failed in your duties, old one.'

The knight began to sing softly, a discordant tune.

'Please don't!'

'It is the punishment,' said the knight. He spun round on his heels and whirled faster around the creature, which was trying to get up.

The third time, the knight stopped and clapped his hands together, bringing his song to an end.

'Sir Mark!' The creature's voice wavered.

'Too late,' said the knight.

The creature shuddered. There was a subtle distending of the air and a rushing noise. The creature held out its long arms to Sir Mark, who sneered and watched as its body shimmered, then vanished.

'Fail in your duty to our Most High Majesty the King,' he said, 'pay the consequences.'

Then, just as the creature had done previously,

he bent down and picked something up from the ground. A shadow. He went to the door, which still hung open in the air. He arranged the shadow into a shape – an unpleasant shape that twitched and huffed and spiked – whispered a few words and fed it through the door.

In the darkness beyond, it took on a life of its own, massing together, slinking off after Simon, Flora and Pike.

And then the young man closed the door with a movement of his hand, a peculiar smile hovering on his mouth; he said a few words, and the outline of the door faded away. 'Well, that was easy,' he said to himself, dusting off his hands. 'It'll get them when they're at their weakest. And I will get my reward.' And he took a pre-rolled cigarette from behind his ear and lit it as he walked away.

The plastic bag blew right over where the door had been.

Chapter Seven

THIS THING
OF DARKNESS

THE FIRST THING that Simon did after he went through the door was to look behind himself. He saw a square of light shining, and then it faded and disappeared.

The door must have shut, he thought, panicked, and ran back to where it had been. Finding nothing there, he turned to where he noticed Flora and Pike were now standing. How would they get back out? His heart was racing. Where were they? Were they in the land of the Broken King? What had the creature said? *Worlds within worlds . . .*

He looked around. They were standing on what

felt like grass, not far from the edge of a lake, which stretched into the distance in front of them as black and still as an oil slick, its surface disturbed only by slivers of silver light from something that looked like a moon hanging above them. Was this the place where his sister was? It looked nothing like the world he'd seen in the visions, all glass towers and black streets and menacing cliffs.

'Doesn't look much like the frozen goods aisle to me,' said Simon, covering up his anxiety with a joke. He found his hand reaching towards Flora, then stopped it. Flora put her arms self-consciously round her shoulders, though it wasn't cold.

'Well, there's a lot of shadows around . . .' said Flora.

The moon – if it was the moon – was high in the sky. It was large and bulbous, and Simon was sure that it was actually giving off light, not merely reflecting it. There was a faint, mushroomy tang in the air.

'Look!' said Flora. There was a tall tree near to them, and hanging from it were similar bone-like structures to the ones they'd seen in the clearing in the woods. But these were glowing dimly, giving off a golden light that seemed about the only warm thing around.

'Let's not separate,' said Simon. 'I don't like the look of that tree.'

'I'm with you there,' said Flora. 'Oh – and you?' She turned her attention to Pike. 'You're the boy who rescued us – from that . . . thing. But – Where's the door, by the way?'

Pike said nothing.

Simon said, 'It's gone. It closed behind us.'

'Then how do we –'

'It'll be OK. I've got the button that opened it before.'

'Well, let's try it now . . .' Flora looked around.

Pike stood still, but Simon could hear something, carried on the continuous breeze. His ears pricked and his heart rose in his chest. Whispers, fragments, phrases.

Simon . . . Do you remember?

Do you remember, Simon?

When me and Daddy and you and Mummy went to the beach . . .

Again on the breeze it came. He stumbled to the side of the lake and didn't hear Flora shouting after him.

. . . the beach, and the kite wouldn't fly, and we ran and ran . . .

It was Anna. It had to be. She was here, somewhere.

Simon ran on, away from Pike and Flora. The grass was black under his feet. He followed the side of the lake, the moonlight showing him a black space far ahead. She was in there somewhere.

I've found her already! he thought, picking up the pace. He imagined his family together again, whole. His parents awake, his sister playing at their feet. He felt the peculiar mixture of longing, shame and love that filled him when he thought about his family.

He ran faster. He pictured her on the beach with the kite, almost being lifted off the ground when there was a gust of strong wind.

The night sky was unclouded. Trees lined the shore of the lake, trees with things hanging down from them that Simon did not bother to stop to look at, with things rustling in them that he did not have time to fear. He was slightly aware of movement, of the wing beats of birds or bats.

Further he ran, and saw a ring of trees. He stopped, panting a little.

There he saw his sister, Anna, in the middle of the ring.

And he also saw himself.

* * *

Flora was still where Simon had left her. Pike was frozen to the spot.

'Did you see where he went?' said Flora, quietly at first, and then louder. 'Did you see where he went?'

But Pike did not move.

'What's your real name?' shouted Flora, shaking him. 'It can't be Pike. Nobody's called Pike.' Flora was suddenly aware that the door was shut behind them. She was feeling very alone. Simon had run off. Who was this boy anyway? What was he doing here?

Pike was staring straight ahead, looking neither to right nor left. He was gazing at a tall black tree with strange, luminous golden fruit. Flora's voice seemed to be sucked up by the giant space around them. She whispered, frightened, 'What's your name? Your real name?'

Then she heard something, seeping into her ears.

. . . they were, like, the best band ever . . .

The sound of her brother's voice galvanized her. *He's here!* she thought. *Johnny!* He was talking about some band that he loved and she hated, but she didn't care now. She shook Pike once more, then leaped in the voice's direction, barely able to prevent herself from screaming out his name.

Johnny, she thought. *Johnny!* She ran through the lattice-work of shadows that the moon cast upon the ground on the other side of the lake from Simon. She came bursting into the same clearing as Simon, but from the opposite side.

She didn't see Simon, though. Who she saw was Johnny, standing with his legs apart, declaiming. His skin was white, as white as the moon, and his face was half in shadow, and he was talking to someone. She didn't stop to see who it was, but instead just ran straight towards him.

Both Simon and Flora sprinted towards their siblings at the same time.

Simon reached Anna.

He didn't notice anything was wrong until just after he'd grabbed her. At first he let out a gasp of surprise and joy, and he held her like a child holds a puppy. He whispered in her ear. 'Anna . . . Anna, I'm so sorry. I'm so happy to see you. I didn't mean it . . .'

All around the shadows stirred and rumbled.

Anna pushed him away and looked at Simon.

Her eyes were black holes, like a full solar eclipse with a corona of fire around the pupils. Her body felt soft and unwieldy, as if made out of some thick

sort of liquid. As if made out of shadow.

'You did mean it, though, didn't you, Simon?'

'What?' said Simon, thrown by her reasonable tone.

'You hurt me. You always hurt me,' she said.

'Anna . . . I . . . Come back, come back with me! Mum and Dad, they're asleep. I came to find you. I didn't mean to send you away. Are you OK?'

'You ruin everything,' said Anna. The words were a shock to Simon. It was the kind of thing he usually said to Anna.

Then Simon noticed the other Simon fully.

'This is my brother,' said Anna.

She held the other Simon's hand, and the other Simon put a protective arm around her shoulders.

Just a few paces away from Simon, but unable to see him, stood Flora, who gazed at another version of herself holding her brother's hand. Her emotions had melted into a curious sort of blankness.

'You always hated me, Flora,' said Johnny. 'Why would you want me to come back? I know you wanted my room. You wanted to get our parents' attention.'

Simon moved. The other Simon moved at the same

time. Simon extended his hand slowly, and saw the other Simon do the same thing. *It's my shadow,* he thought. *A Shadow Simon.*

Flora stepped forwards, and the Shadow Flora edged towards her. Then Flora saw that she was connected to the other Flora. In fact, it looked like the other Flora was actually *coming* from her, in the way that a shadow does when the sun is low.

Flora was struck by her own selfishness. She'd never tried to help Johnny, not really. She'd let him fester, fall apart. She had failed him. She found her body weakening. The Shadow Flora drew nearer to her.

Simon looked at the Shadow Simon. *I'm so weak,* he thought, *and vain. I only ever thought about myself. I never thought what it might be like to be her, did I?*

The Shadow Simon inched forwards. Simon remembered something he'd learned at school about matter and anti-matter. Didn't they explode when they met, cancel each other out?

I'm useless, thought Simon. He saw Anna gazing blankly at him.

* * *

Flora fell to her knees. She could sense annihilation in herself. *Why is Johnny smiling?* she thought.

Beyond them, the thing that the Knight of the Swan had poured through the door was rustling and forming. It took shape, circling around the clearing so that it created a black barrier.

It was like a snake, like the snake in books that eats its own tail – except that it seemed to have no distinct head – although its attention was definitely directed towards Simon and Flora.

Simon was dimly aware of it, felt a sense of oppression. Flora's head was bowed.

The black ring of smoke and shadow grew tighter around them.

Now Simon dropped to his knees. He could not look himself in the eye. The Shadow Simon reached out a hand. He could feel his own death in it.

Flora felt her skin grow cold.

Some spark of self-awareness remained in Flora's heart. *That can't be Johnny,* she thought. *He would never smile like that, with that look, that horrible look in his eyes, at my pain. He loved me, I know. I remember he did. He wouldn't be like that.*

* * *

Looking at Anna's blank face, Simon thought none of those things. He bowed to the knowledge that he was nothing, that he would become nothing. He could feel himself getting smaller and smaller, disappearing, vanishing.

Flora looked up, saw herself advancing, saw the blackness in the Shadow Flora's eyes. Heard Johnny laughing.

He wouldn't laugh like that, she thought. *It's not him.*

Then, stronger still. *It's not him.*

But – and this was the hardest thing to admit – *that thing is me. That thing of darkness and shadow is me. It's a part of me. I should not be afraid of it.*

I should accept it.

Slowly, she felt strength returning. She made herself stand up.

The Shadow Flora kept coming towards her, its fingers nearly reaching her now.

She called up the deepest reserves of her courage, remembered Johnny when he was younger and used to play her the records he loved. 'You're not Johnny,' she said, quietly at first. Then her voice rang out. 'You're not Johnny!' Warmth surged through her

body. 'I know who I am. I'm Flora.' She reached out her hand to touch the Shadow Flora. 'I'm ready for you!'

Her fingertips met those of the Shadow Flora.

Flora screamed with pain. It was like an electric shock. All her faults and weaknesses poured through her mind. Every shameful thing she'd ever done, every lie she'd told, every cowardly or stupid thing came back to her, all at once in a hideous avalanche.

But she didn't let it overcome her. She stood strong. 'You can't eat me,' she shouted. 'I am Flora! I eat the shadow! I am Flora. I eat the shadow! I am the shadow!'

Her dark self merged with her – powerful, strong, about to submerge her for ever.

Not this time, she said, and pushed against it with her mind as hard as she could.

And then she felt herself assuming it, consuming it. Another flood of memories overwhelmed her. Stealing things to get her parents' attention. Blaming Johnny. Every embarrassing and awkward moment of her life came rushing over her at once. It felt like she was being torn in two. With a huge effort of will, she brought herself together. *It's me*, she thought. *It's all me. Just take it, accept it, overcome it.*

And then she breathed. The feelings ebbed away. She saw she was in a clearing. The Shadow Johnny had vanished, and with him the Shadow Flora.

She understood what had happened. *You have to accept yourself,* she thought. You have to take the darkness and make it your own.

And then she saw in front of her a small, round, black object. She bent down towards it. It was a sphere, perfectly black and perfectly shiny. She saw her reflection in it, even though there was no light, and she knew what it was. *It's me,* she thought. *It's my shadow.* She picked it up and held it, smooth and odd in her fingers, before pocketing it.

She looked up and saw the wall of blackness closing in from the edge of the clearing. *What on earth is that?* she thought. Her heart started to pound. It moved like it was alive. Smoky and shimmery and alive. It was a snake, made out of shadows. A shadowsnake.

She felt the malice coming off it. Saw it inching towards her. Saw things that might have been mouths, teeth, eyes, shimmering in its blackness. She saw a limb reach out of it and graze the grass beneath. The grass smoked and burned, and as the tendril grazed her, she felt a sting of pain on her

arm. Instinctively she put a hand to it, and looked about for an exit. There was none. She was trapped.

She spun round on her heels, desperately seeking a way out. There must be something. As she looked, she noticed that the shadow wasn't entirely solid — there were gaps in it where it shivered and broke apart. They didn't open for very long, though. Sometimes they were big enough to get through, and sometimes they were only tiny.

She had to act quickly. How could she get out? She would have to run through one of the gaps. But how? What if the shadowsnake folded in on her? Would she burn like the grass?

Then she saw Simon, down on his knees. He was rocking gently, back and forth. It looked like he was having trouble breathing. He was coughing.

A dark claw passed above her head.

Flora ran to Simon, grabbed him by the shoulders, saw that his eyes were rolling into the back of his head. *I need to get through to him*, thought Flora. She shook him but it made no difference.

The shadowsnake was tightening its circle. Now limbs, beaks and claws were darting out of it, snaking over their heads, around their bodies. It was playing with them, as if they were nothing more than toys.

'Simon!' she called. 'It's going to kill us . . . You have to snap out of it!'

Simon was not aware at all of Flora. All he could see was Anna, the blankness on her face, and his own shadowself coming forwards with a smile.

I failed you, Anna, he thought. *Now you'll be gone, and I'll be gone as well.*

He remembered, then, his mother's face. Imagined his parents sitting alone together by the fireplace with the frayed carpet and the empty chairs.

Yes, thought Simon. *Yes.*

His head snapped up.

That's what I've got to do.

Flora stepped back.

'Anna!' he shouted. 'I've come to find you.'

He stood up. The Shadow Simon kept coming towards him. He knew what he had to do. It was the command of the messengers, the first task set by the Broken King. *Eat the shadow.* Consume it. Make it part of yourself.

He braced himself, reached out his arms and embraced his shadowself. *I don't know what will happen to me,* he thought. *But I'm ready for it.*

Simon shuddered. It was like being dipped into the iciest waters. He roared and raged with anguish and

pain, with all the repressed hatreds and annoyances of his life. He howled into the air.

'I am the darkness!' he yelled. 'I am the darkness, and the darkness is me!'

When he had finished, he was quiet. And then he saw that he was standing beside Flora. There was a round, black object on the grass in front of him.

'No time to talk,' said Flora, pointing. 'Pick that up. We've got to get away . . .'

The body of the shadowsnake had now grown so that it almost seemed to touch the sky. A head coiled out of it. It looked like the shadowbeast they'd seen in the forest, and it rolled its way towards Flora and Simon. Other heads, other limbs, began to grow. There was a low, hissing noise.

'What do we do?' said Simon. He felt stronger now too, ready to face anything.

'I think I know,' said Flora. She'd met the darkness in herself. She'd taken it in. She was braver, now, that was true. But there was also another side. *Eat the shadow.* What did that mean? She thought she'd worked it out. 'Remember? *Eat the shadow.* A positive and a negative. What do they make?' She pressed Simon's shoulder.

'Is this a good time for a maths lesson?' said

Simon nervously. A snaky limb rushed past them, grazing him. It stung unexpectedly, opening up a rip in his T-shirt. Fear coursed in his veins. 'We've got to get out of here!' The shadowsnake brushed past his other shoulder and he winced with the pain.

'What do they make?' said Flora urgently.

Simon thought desperately. 'They cancel each other out.'

'They make nothing. *Eat the shadow.* The disguise. That's what we have now. Invisibility.' She held out the sphere in her hand, and Simon did the same.

'How do we make it work?' He felt all round it as another limb oozed by Simon's head. He saw one approaching Flora from behind and dragged her out of the way.

Another head appeared from out of the shadowy gloom. It was larger, and it had eyes that glowed green and orange and blue before turning silver. It regarded them loftily, as if deciding on the best way to destroy them.

'We have the strength to be invisible now,' said Simon. 'That's it.' He looked at the sphere again and twisted it.

The top half came off. Inside were six smaller spheres.

'I guess we eat them?' said Simon.

'We don't really have much choice!' shouted Flora.

The shadowsnake was swerving its heads from side to side, looking as if it were about to pounce.

'Here goes!' Simon picked up one of the little black spheres, popped it into his mouth and swallowed.

Flora watched in astonishment as Simon vanished. 'Can you hear me?' she heard him say. She felt him poke her in the ribs. She took a sphere from her own, and swallowed it down. She looked up and was surprised to now see Simon's outline.

The two snakeheads lashed out. Flora and Simon jumped back.

'It can't see us,' shouted Flora jubilantly.

The snakeheads were looking around, confused. The gaps in itself grew larger as it stretched to poke and sniff in different directions.

'Now come on,' she said. 'Let's run!'

They watched as a beastly head tore one way, and another head the other. As soon as a gap formed between them, Simon and Flora immediately ran through it.

The shadowsnake howled in rage continuing to search for what it couldn't see. Flora and Simon raced back down the side of the lake. The creature

pursued them, sniffing the air. Grass and trees and bushes burned up behind it, but it was dashing its heads in the wrong directions, hitting the lake, splashing the cold black water all over them.

'I see Pike!' said Simon.

There he was, still frozen, exactly where they had left him. There was the tree with the gnarled trunk. There were the golden, shivering bone-scrolls.

'But how do we get back out?'

They reached Pike. Simon shouted his name. Behind them the shadowsnake sensed Pike and headed towards them.

'Quick!'

'We're invisible,' said Flora. 'Pike can't see us!'

'Oh yes,' said Simon. 'Can he hear us?'

Simon went up to Pike and shouted at him. Pike didn't move.

'How do we switch back?'

'The spheres!'

They took one more sphere each and swallowed them. Pain spread from Simon's stomach all the way through his body. Flora came back into view suddenly, clutching her midriff.

The shadowsnake was racing towards them. They felt a strange power coming from it – malicious and

deadly. The shadowsnake extended itself forwards. Its mouths were legion now. It was all gaping jaws and staring eyes. It stretched and billowed and yawned – and stirred Pike from his reverie. He came back to his senses and saw what was happening, saw it coming towards him, saw Simon and Flora. He looked around, and saw the golden things hanging from the tree. They reminded him of something.

The shadowsnake lashed in their direction, then coiled itself in, ready for another strike.

'I know what to do,' said Pike quickly. He went to the tree without saying anything, and reached up to touch the golden things hanging from it.

The shadowsnake was getting closer. A beastly head was nearing them.

The golden scroll Pike had touched opened slowly at first, then faster, and then with speed like a flame on a piece of paper, the rest of them unfolded and reformed into what Simon could see were men and women. *The messengers said there would be people trapped in here*, he thought.

One of the men shouted out a joyful cry. 'We are released!'

They saw Pike, Flora and Simon, and then the shadowsnake.

'The work of the Broken King!' cried a woman.

Quickly the golden people formed a line and moved forwards. They held their hands together and their brightness grew in power.

The shadowsnake recoiled. A tendril poked its way towards Simon. He jumped towards Pike.

'The button!' shouted Flora.

'Where's the door?' shouted Simon.

Pike said, 'I can see it. There's the edge.'

Simon got the button out and felt for the impression. There it was. He pushed the button in.

The shadowsnake swooped at the golden line.

The door opened. The white light from the other side was almost blinding.

Simon stood back. 'Go!'

Flora went through first, then Pike, then Simon.

'Keep the door open!' called one of the golden people.

Looking back through, Simon, Flora and Pike saw their brightness expand. They heard the howl of the shadowsnake, the sound of a beast in great distress. And then they heard nothing.

They stood panting on the other side, back in the loading bay. Flora and Simon were soaking with sweat and water from the lake. Pike was freezing

cold, his skin icy to the touch.

'How did you . . . ?' asked Simon.

Pike said nothing for a moment. And then he said, 'I saw you in the clearing by the stone circle. Those weird things on the tree. They looked like the same thing. I thought it might help.'

'You've been watching us since then?'

Pike nodded.

'And the door?'

Pike shrugged. 'I don't know. I could just see it.'

Simon took hold of his shoulder. 'Why are you following us?'

Pike kept his mouth shut. Simon was about to press him further when five little points of light, golden and thrilling, came through the door and grew and expanded until they became five people – four men and one woman. They were dressed in flowing golden robes, as the people on the bird-deer had been, but they seemed more human somehow. Their faces were not gold. The woman had long black hair, and the men had manes of gold. One of the men turned and closed the door that still lay open with a single gesture.

'Nothing will trouble us from there,' he said.

'Who are you?' asked Simon slowly.

'You have released us,' they said as one, and bowed to Simon, Flora and Pike.

'We were imprisoned,' said the black-haired woman. 'We are travellers between the worlds. We are from the Golden Realm. We planned to visit the Kingdom before it . . . before the king became as he is now. We have long been kept in that place against our will. An empty place, where nothing grows or lives.'

Simon said, 'So that's not the Kingdom?'

'It is not. It is a holding space, somewhere that is in between.'

Simon thought, *Like where my parents are.* 'It wasn't me who set you free, it was . . .' He pointed to Pike.

'Pike,' said Pike, then immediately wished he hadn't.

The black-haired woman looked strangely at Pike, and shook her head. *It's like she can't quite see him*, thought Simon. *What is he?*

'We will come for you,' said the woman and smiled. 'We will watch you and help you as far as we are able. We give you thanks.'

Their brightness dimmed and then they had vanished, leaving the three of them standing in the

deserted loading bay at the back of the supermarket.

'Pike,' said Flora, turning to look at him.

The boy stood there, slightly chubby cheeks reddened, sweat pouring off him, his clothes loose and baggy. 'Yes,' said Pike simply.

'You've got to tell us who you are . . .'

'I –' began Pike.

'What's going on round here, then?' said another voice.

They all turned to see a man in a supermarket uniform lugging a box of onions. 'You shouldn't be round here!'

Simon quickly put his sunglasses back on. Thank God they were still in his pocket.

'Nothing!' said Flora sweetly. 'My brother here just had a bit of an accident, but it's OK now. Come on, then, time to go home.'

She led the way cheerfully, suppressing the fear and terror that had risen in her heart, and the questions that loomed in her mind about Pike. Simon followed, nodding politely to the supermarket man.

When he was outside in the sunshine again he felt like stopping and embracing the world. But instead, he skulked after Flora, just behind Pike, as the sun boiled down from the sky.

* * *

In a café nearby, the Knight of the Swan was sitting drinking a cappuccino, thinking. He allowed his mind to empty itself sometimes. The darkness that lay in there was sometimes too hard for even him to bear.

As he sat there, a movement caught his eye. He looked around. The waitress was facing the other way, pouring tea into a mug for a man in a high-vis jacket. Nobody had come in for a while. The only other person in the café was an elderly lady in a bright blue suit reading the *Daily Telegraph*.

Sir Mark held out his hand. A small shadow detached itself from a larger one and moved towards him, although anybody watching wouldn't have noticed it, had they seen it, since things like that don't happen in real life, only in the pages of books.

The shadow must have communicated something to him, on some frequency or wavelength that human ears could not detect. It was something that Sir Mark did not like, and his face darkened.

He frowned, steepled his fingers together, and stared into the distance.

Flora, Simon and Pike were sitting behind some

bushes not far from the supermarket. Flora and Simon had, unconsciously, huddled together, and Pike was a little way away from them, his back to a tree trunk. In the golden sunlight he looked pasty and unwell. His cheeks were hollow and his eyes gummy. Simon noticed that Pike's fingernails were so encrusted with dirt that it didn't look like they'd ever been cleaned. Then he looked down at his own. They were not much better.

It seemed to Simon that there were a lot of things that they needed to work out with Pike. Who was he? Where had he come from so suddenly? Why had he frozen in the holding place? He'd rescued them by the tent from the night-creature, that was true, but when they were truly in danger from the shadowsnake he'd gone stiff. Then, on the other hand, he'd woken up the prisoners. What did Pike know?

Simon stood up suddenly. 'Who are you?' he said in a tone that sounded more unfriendly than he had meant it. Flora put out a restraining hand, but he ignored it.

Pike sat wrapped in layers of his own thoughts. He was dimly aware of Simon standing up and shouting at him. Pike stood up too. He said the only

thing he knew to say when confronted in such a way.

'Pike. I'm Pike.'

'But what kind of a name is that? Don't you have a first name?'

'First name?' said Pike.

'Look,' said Simon, calming himself down. 'We've been in danger – twice. Once you saved us – and once you didn't.'

'I freed the prisoners. You would have been killed. We all would have been killed.'

'That's true, Simon,' said Flora.

'But how did you know how to do it? Did you watch us when we were in the clearing? How do we know you're not one of the Broken King's agents? You could be leading us astray!'

'I'm not,' said Pike simply.

'He doesn't know how to lie,' said Flora.

'How do you know?'

'Look at him.'

Pike was staring straight ahead of himself, his fists clenched a little.

'I don't know,' said Pike.

'What do you mean? Why don't you both sit down?' Flora pulled Simon down next to her, and Pike squatted, his haunches quivering visibly.

'I don't know. The answers to your questions. I don't know who I am.'

'What about your parents?' asked Flora.

'I don't remember.'

'Where did you grow up?' she tried.

He paused before he said, 'Everywhere,' and then chewed his fingernails. 'I know things about the woods. I can steal things from the towns. Nobody bothers me and I don't bother them. Until you came along.' He said the last few words violently, and a little sadly.

'So are you on their side?' asked Simon.

'I want to help you.'

He didn't answer the question, thought Simon. He drew Flora aside. 'What shall we do about him?'

'I think we should stick with him.'

'He doesn't know anything about himself! He might be dangerous. I don't want anything to get in the way of finding Anna. When I saw her there, I felt . . .'

'I felt it too, Simon. I saw Johnny.'

They stared mutely at each other. The trees rustled overhead.

'If we don't let him come with us, he'll probably follow us anyway,' whispered Flora. 'He doesn't look

like he's got anywhere else to go, does he? We'll just keep a close eye on him. And he is pretty helpful.'

Simon was grappling with conflicting thoughts. It was bad enough that he had Flora with him; now they would have to take this strange boy with them too. Looking at Pike, he saw someone who could be a potential enemy. But he also saw his saviour – twice over, now. Grudgingly, he held out his hand to Pike.

'All right, then, Pike,' said Simon. 'You're on.'

Chapter Eight

THE KNIGHT
OF THE SWAN

SIMON FELT THE warmth that he associated
with the messengers filling him, but he could
not see them anywhere. It came and went very
quickly. When it had disappeared, he sensed the
presence of something hot in his hand. He uncurled
his fingers slowly.

They had walked further into the woods by the
side of the road, off the path, and set up camp
under the arching shade of a large oak tree. It was
evening, and they were all exhausted. The tent was
too small for all three of them, so they'd devised a
system of rotation where one of them sat outside

to keep watch whilst the other two slept or rested.

Simon was on his own, sitting outside. He stared at what lay in his palm.

It was a little golden bird-deer, a miniature of the ones the messengers rode. It shook its head. He felt its tiny hooves tickle his skin.

'Where did you come from?' he said quietly. He wondered if the released prisoners had left it with him, but then it had only just seemed to appear, hadn't it?

Flora must have heard him; her voice murmured from inside the tent. Her body followed soon afterwards, and she poked her head out into the fresh air, her hair lying lank, some of it plastered against her cheek. Simon carefully hid the little bird-deer, and felt it snuggle down into his pocket. He didn't want to share it with Flora, feeling it was something that had been sent just for him. What its purpose was he would consider later.

'We should be thinking about the second task,' said Flora.

'We should be thinking about Pike,' said Simon.

Flora sighed. 'He's all right, you know, I'm sure of it. I mean, he rescued us twice.' Her face brightened. 'It doesn't look like carelessness, does it?'

'What?' said Simon.

'Never mind,' said Flora, her face falling again. 'You'll do it at school some day.'

Something snapped in Simon. 'You're patronising me again.'

Flora looked up quickly. 'No, Simon, I – it's a play, you know, Oscar Wilde . . .'

'Steal the sun,' said Simon, talking over her and looking away from her face pale with tiredness. She was a mess. He wondered what he must look like. He felt again a tug of something he did not want to admit and turned his thoughts back to the message.

What could it possibly mean? He gazed up into the sky, shading his eyes against the glare. He remembered his dream, the boiling sphere, the jets shooting out of it, the weirdness of the light and the heat. He remembered the vision the messengers had given them. The shadow – that was disguise, Flora had worked that out. But what was the sun? A jet? A spear? A weapon?

'Shall we look at the map?' asked Simon.

Flora had got out of the tent and was standing up a few paces away from him, stretching.

Simon looked in his bag for the skin-map, found it, and laid it on the scrubby grass where he unrolled it.

It had returned to its original empty state. Simon felt in his pockets for the porcupine spine, and held his hand over the map once more. He pricked his finger, and watched as a small drop of blood fell on to the map. He wrote the words, *Steal the sun* and waited.

Nothing happened.

'Try again,' said Flora, who was standing near to him now, bending over his shoulder. Her hair grazed Simon's cheek and tickled it. They could hear Pike's breathing from inside the tent, slow and steady.

'It does hurt, you know,' said Simon, pricking his finger again. Once more the blood fell. Once more he wrote the words. Once more the map stayed inert.

'Let me try,' said Flora impatiently, taking the spine from Simon. She pricked her finger – at first unsuccessfully, then she succeeded, but rather harder than she'd meant to. She opened up a good long rip on the soft pad of her finger, so that a large drop of blood fell on to the map. She wrote, slowly and carefully, sucking her finger afterwards, *STEAL THE SUN*.

But still nothing changed.

Inside the tent Pike snorted and rolled over; the movement woke him up, and he poked his tousled head out of the tent.

'Whazgoinon?' he said.

'Go back to sleep,' said Flora, a little sadly.

Pike fell back inside immediately.

The other two sat facing each other, staring at the map till the shadows started to lengthen.

Simon felt the tiny winged deer stir in his pocket and guiltily covered it. Maybe it held the clue? But he was too shy of it for the moment, and too pleased that it had come to him alone, so he kept quiet.

'What about the shadow creatures?' asked Flora as the sky grew darker. She shivered at the thought of what might be hiding in the night.

'I think they'll leave us alone tonight,' said Simon, the moon tinting his features with silver.

Simon was right, although he wouldn't have known why.

A few miles away from where Flora, Simon and Pike had pitched their tent, the Knight of the Swan was standing by the side of a small pond. There was nothing particularly unusual about the sight of a young man idling there, only that it was dusk, and Sir Mark was naked. A pair of swans was gliding in circles, their huge ungainly feet powering away unseen under their elegant bodies.

He appeared entranced, staring intently at the surface of the water as if he were a hunter trying to catch the slipperiest of fish. The shadows on his white flesh would have resembled tribal tattoos, if they didn't have the nasty habit of moving and sliding around on the surface of his skin. He was tall and thin; his body tapered into a narrow waist. With his long legs and arms he resembled nothing so much as a stork.

The shadows on his body heaved and sighed and then drew together until they covered his whole body. He opened his mouth. It was a myth, he thought, that swans only sang at the moment of their death. It was also a myth that their song is harmonious. From his lips issued a sound that was harsh and discordant, full of clashing dissonances.

The two swans drew nearer to him, and they too opened their beaks to make the same sound. They parted and made a circle with their wakes, into which Sir Mark stepped without looking down.

And then he was not there at all.

Now he stood in front of a glass table in a long room with white walls and a huge window that looked out on to blackness. Lights shone out brilliantly, set in long rows along the ceiling high, high above

him. The shadows on his body had made Sir Mark a garment of sorts. He stood with it flapping around him, bowing his head slightly to the two people who sat at the far end of the table on shining metal chairs.

One of them was a girl. She sat with her hands steepled together, leaning forwards with an expression of calm immutability, her black hair tied back behind her head. She was the Silver Princess, the eldest daughter of the king. The other was a man older than Sir Mark, who sat upright, hands in his lap. The tip of a ceremonial sword poked out from behind the table. *The Lord Chancellor*, Sir Mark thought. The chancellor looked nervous and the knight watched him take a sip from the glass that stood on the table before he spoke. He offered none to the knight.

'Is it a declaration of war?' said the chancellor.

Sir Mark smoothly shook his head. 'Not yet, though the prisoners were released from the holding place.'

'The boy and the girl – Flora and Simon – they seek the Blessed Ones?'

The knight smiled. 'Most certainly. They wish to retract their desires. They want to bring their siblings back from His Majesty. They do not know, though, what they are getting involved with.'

'They escaped the shadowsnake?' This was the princess. From somewhere not far distant there came the sound of a great roar of people. It rumbled through the long room. The glass of the windows shook in its frames.

'There's a . . . Taking Apart,' said the chancellor, in explanation of the noise.

Sir Mark's expression flickered briefly. 'Who is it?'

'Nobody important,' said the Princess. Sir Mark watched her face closely. She did not move a single muscle on her face. *Such determination*, he thought. *A true daughter of a king.*

'It was the Black Knight,' said the chancellor.

This was shocking enough, but Sir Mark, still watching the princess, kept his face as calm as he could. Whatever they said he'd show no emotion, none at all. *I am a servant of the king*, he thought, and glanced covertly at the princess.

'To return to my question,' said the chancellor, as the roars died away to be replaced with the quiet buzz of the lights above them. 'They escaped the shadowsnake? With the help of the Realm?'

'They freed the prisoners, yes,' said Sir Mark reluctantly. 'They also managed to kill one of the royal hounds.'

'How did they do that? Surely impossible!'

'They had help,' replied the knight.

'Who from?'

Sir Mark tapped his long, white finger against the hollow of his cheek. 'Unknown,' he said. 'The Realm did not help them kill the hound, and they freed the prisoners themselves too.'

The princess looked up sharply, levelling her gaze at Mark who stood up straighter feeling it on him. 'How did they escape from the shadowsnake?'

Mark paused before speaking. The buzz of the lights filled his ears. *I must remain calm*, he thought. 'I think they . . . ate the shadow.'

The princess's coldness was more frightening than her fury would have been.

'You're close to the end, Knight of the Swan,' she said. She unsheathed the sword from the scabbard of the chancellor with a quick and forceful movement, and drew back her hand as if she were about to let fly with a javelin. Sir Mark saw a bead of light glinting at the tip of it. He saw death in the sword.

A second passed and the sword landed, quivering, in the folds of the knight's robes, an inch from his foot. Casually, he put his hand to it, pulled it out, and placed it on the table, the handle facing towards the princess.

'I will use other methods,' he said.

'The king —' said the princess.

'Will be displeased. I know,' said Sir Mark. 'There is aught that I can do.' His voice had turned to the courtly tones of old that they had long since ceased to use since the troubles had started and the king had taken the Blessed again. He bowed, his head almost touching the table top.

The princess waved a hand, as if she were wafting away a not particularly irritating fly, and Sir Mark, the Knight of the Swan, was gone.

The princess moved to the window and looked out at the avenue below. It was lined with rushing people dressed in blacks and greys, clear in the night light that came from the tall white lamps that lined the avenues. Above, she saw the dark moon, then turned her gaze back down.

She winced inside, keeping her expression stony as she saw the armoured soldiers marching down the centre of the road. The trees were frilled with the remnants of Taking Aparts. She turned away as she saw the mortal remains of the Black Knight hung up. There was now barely a branch without its grisly ornamentation.

'My Lord Chancellor,' she said imperiously to the

quivering man. 'Prepare my mount. I ride to see my father.'

'As you will, my lady,' said the chancellor, who almost tripped over getting up from the table and walking out backwards.

The fool, thought the princess. But she kept her face straight and nodded politely to him. *One wrong word,* she thought, *and even I might be killed . . . I am playing a dangerous game.* She let the terrible idea hang in her mind, then turned to follow the chancellor.

'Pass my jacket over,' said Flora to Simon. It had stopped raining and it was early in the morning. Neither of them had watches but Simon, judging by a very vague recollection of something he'd learned at school about the position of the sun, thought it was past six o'clock. Pike was still asleep. The two of them were sitting with their backs to a tree trunk. Simon, who was munching on a biscuit, shrugged and reached for the jacket.

As he passed it across, something fell out of it. Simon picked it up, saying, 'You dropped this.'

Flora snatched quickly at it, and something about her expression made Simon hold his hand back out of her reach.

'What is it?'

'Give it here!'

'Wait! Ow!' Simon uncurled his fingers. Inside his palm was what he thought must be a hospital syringe. He couldn't think why Flora would want to carry around something like that. Maybe she had diabetes. In which case, it made it all the worse that she was coming along with him. They'd have to worry about insulin injections all the time. He said, as quietly as he could, 'I didn't know, I'm sorry.'

'How could you know?' said Flora.

Simon was amazed to see that she was crying. He gulped a little and put his arm around her shoulders. They felt warm and comfortable and he edged closer to her.

'It's all right,' said Simon, surprised at himself. 'We'll . . . steal from a chemist's or something. '

'Don't say that!' said Flora, pushing him away. 'Do you think I . . . ? Do you think . . . What do you think?' Her anger forced its way out of her throat.

'Well, I didn't know diabetics were grumpy as well,' said Simon.

'Diabetics?' said Flora. 'Diabetics . . . Oh, I see. No. No, it's not that at all.'

'Well, what is it, then? Why have you got a syringe?'

Flora grabbed both her knees as if they were a child she was holding back from a cliff edge.

'It's why I'm here,' she said, deflated. 'It's Johnny's jacket. His leather jacket that he always wore. It smells of him. He was a drug addict.'

Simon didn't know what to say so he said the only thing he could, which was nothing.

Flora continued. 'I love him so much, but when he was on drugs he was like a . . . I remember once seeing him when he'd dosed up. He was sitting on the sofa, our parents were away, and his eyes were rolling into the back of his head. I was so much younger than him I thought he was a monster. I screamed and screamed and he did nothing . . . I'd steal from him. I suppose I thought that if I stole his money then he wouldn't have any to buy drugs. But he used to steal from other people. That's why he was sent down from Cambridge, because he was caught stealing off his flatmate. And then he came home and my mother spent the whole day just worshipping him, telling him it was all right, and I couldn't take it . . .'

'That's why we're here. Both of us,' said Simon. 'That's why I've got this,' he said, pointing to the welt on his cheek. 'It's a punishment, I think. For being . . .

for being mean to Anna. For not being there for her.'
He felt released when he said it.

'Me too,' said Flora. And, sighing, she showed
Simon her calf. 'The messenger whipped my leg too.
It's selfishness, isn't it? Do you think . . . Do you
think that's why they were taken?'

'That rhyme,' said Simon. 'I hadn't thought of
it for years and then suddenly it came to me that
night. Why do you think that is?'

'I don't know – but it was the same for me. I don't
really know why I did it. It was almost like . . .'

'Like someone else was making you do it?'

'Yes!' said Flora.

'I mean, I wanted it to happen. I really did, when
I read it.'

'Me too,' said Flora. 'Me too . . .'

Shame and guilt overcame Simon. 'But I think
there's something else going on, something bigger
. . . The Broken King, what can you remember about
him?'

'Nothing really,' said Flora.

'And the Golden Realm? We've seen how they use
light, and the Broken Kingdom uses darkness. And
we, I guess, are in-between.'

'I guess so,' said Flora.

'Well, let's sort out the map, then,' said Simon, pondering.

Pike snorted in his sleep as they unrolled the map and stared at it. It had reverted to the blank state it had been in when they'd found it.

'It changed when I wrote with the porcupine spine Anna gave me,' said Simon. 'With my blood, I mean.'

'Of course,' said Anna. 'The needle!'

'What if it's been . . . used?' said Simon.

Flora picked it up and looked it over. 'I don't think it has. I mean, it looks clean, don't you think? Is there any antiseptic left in that first aid kit? I think it's in the tent . . .'

'Don't wake up Pike,' said Simon, a little too quickly. He didn't want Pike in on this. It felt too private.

'Chill out,' said Flora. She ducked into the tent and emerged a second later with the kit, and quickly found the antiseptic. She applied it briskly. 'Right.' She rolled up her sleeve and then her face fell, aware that she was making a horrible parody of her brother's addiction. She held the needle to her index finger, pricked it, and they both watched expectantly as the blood fell.

She formed the letters carefully, until she had written, *STEAL THE SUN.*

Immediately the map formed lines and contours.

Simon shook his head. 'I don't recognise this at all,' he said. 'It looks like it's zoomed out. You know, like on the internet when you click and it pans back like a camera.'

'I do know,' said Flora. 'That is exactly what it's done.' She threw a quick glance at Simon. 'Can you drive?'

Taken aback, Simon said, 'Well, no, not exactly. I mean, I've held the steering wheel a couple of times but . . . can you?'

'I can actually. It's one of the few things Johnny bothered to teach me, so I could pick him up from the station when I'm seventeen, no doubt,' she added to herself.

'Why do you ask?'

Flora pointed at the map. 'Look. The direction we need to go in is the same: north. It's just the scale that's different. Which means that from here we're going to . . .'

'Where?'

It was Pike's voice. He'd woken up and was half-hanging out of the tent, gazing blearily at them. He came out of the tent and stood up, folding his arms, not catching the eye of either Flora or Simon.

They turned, wild and jumpy, Simon irritated at being interrupted and Flora trying to hide the same feeling.

'In the dark,' said Pike, and then stopped, unable to give voice to his thoughts.

'Yes?' said Simon, more unkindly than he'd meant.

'In the dark,' continued Pike, now more to spite Simon. 'When I was frozen, it was because . . .' He faltered again.

Flora shot a warning look at Simon, and as encouragingly as she could said, 'What is it, Pike?'

He shuffled his feet. Simon caught a sudden whiff of Pike's raw smell and wrinkled his nose.

'I saw . . . things.'

Simon laughed. 'So did we all.'

'Shut up, Simon,' said Flora quietly.

'I saw,' said Pike, faster now, 'I saw you.' He pointed at Simon. 'And you,' indicating Flora. 'And you were . . .' His voice was full of a terrible urgency.

'What?' said Simon, genuinely concerned, watching Pike's face contort.

'You were *empty*.'

The word fell flat into the air. Pike, ashamed, watched the two of them, their faces uncomprehending.

Simon said, 'Well, it doesn't matter anyway. We're

off.' Without another word he began to take the tent down, struggling a little with the poles. Flora soon joined him, but Pike stood, wavering under a tree, and when they were ready he followed just a few steps behind.

He'd seen them, when he'd been standing by that tree with the golden people. He'd seen them in a vision. They'd been on a cart, pulled by something nameless, led by a hooded figure through glittering streets with tall shining black towers soaring up on either side, and the moon – always the moon – hanging low in the sky. He'd seen Flora and Simon right up close in the cart, lolling and bound. If he'd reached out he might have been able to touch them. But it wasn't them at all. Their faces were empty, their eyes expressionless, as if they'd had their entire essence taken from them.

Looking at their backs now, he could only think of what he'd seen.

He tramped on, regardless. He had to tell them. He had to protect them now. He would have to warn them before it happened. Because he knew that when it did happen, it would mean the end.

Chapter Nine

RAVEN

AND THE FLAMES

'LOST YOUR TICKETS, you say?' The ticket seller was peering at Flora, Simon and Pike through the plastic barrier that was his protection against the hordes. He was rheumatic, and his wife had left him that morning for a bus driver from Uxminster. He had no patience for lying children.

Flora put on her best polite voice. Pike and Simon were skulking behind her, Simon wearing his sunglasses, Pike as still as a frightened deer. He hated railway stations; in fact, wasn't even really sure that he knew what they were.

'Yes,' continued Flora. 'My brothers and I are on

our way home to London. But we've lost our tickets and we've only got ten pounds between us.'

'Brothers, eh?' He took in the well-dressed, if slightly grubby-looking Flora; the tracksuited Pike with his pale, blotchy face; and the skinny, nervous Simon. He looked at the queue forming behind them and sighed.

'Cousins, I meant,' said Flora, following his gaze. 'I mean, I call them brothers, but really they're cousins.'

'Sorry, love,' said the ticket seller.

Flora was about to complain when an office worker pushed past them and asked loudly for a return to London, so she led the two boys off the station forecourt.

'Well, that didn't work,' said Simon. 'What do we do now?'

As they traipsed off, something stirred in the ticket seller's mind. That boy – the pudgy one. He'd seen him before, loitering around – he was sure he'd been pickpocketing, or shoplifting from the news outlet. It was probably all a con. They were in some gang or other, trying to get money out of people. He pulled down the half-curtain that showed his cubicle was closed, causing much of the waiting line

to complain, and went outside to give the boy a piece of his mind.

A man in the queue turned to watch him go. He was tall and black-suited, although the suit seemed to shiver like a shadow.

Flora, Simon and Pike were standing huddled just by the entrance, trying to work out how they were going to get to London without any money and with no means of transport. The ticket seller assumed his authoritarian face – the kind he used when he was dealing with ticketless teenage boys; the kind he'd like to have used that morning with his wife – and tapped Pike, self-importantly, on the shoulder and cleared his throat.

They all turned, saw the ticket seller – and saw, behind him, the man in the shadowy black suit.

At first they stood still, as in a tableau. Then Simon whispered, 'That's the Knight of the Swan – he attacked me at home. We shouldn't stick around.'

Simon started to back away, and then to run. Flora and Pike came after him as quickly as they could. They ran in unspoken agreement, away from the ticket seller, away from the Knight.

'Hey!' called the ticket seller.

It was hard going with the rucksack and tent but

Simon found he could easily keep pace with Pike, who hid surprising speed under his faint podginess. Flora's long, ungainly legs moved in a blur, her brother's leather jacket flapping out after her.

They turned the corner of the station and came out on a side road blocked up with traffic trying to get in or out of the town. Behind them, the ticket seller, who was imagining reclaiming his wife by telling her a heroic story about how he'd bested a gang of teenagers and won, was forgetting his rheumatism and rediscovering his youth.

Simon, Flora and Pike were kept back from crossing the road by the whoosh of cars. They dithered on the kerb.

He's recognised me, thought Simon, pushing his sunglasses up on to his nose. This was dangerous. What would the knight do? They had to escape. But how?

There were no gaps in the cars for them to get through. The ticket seller was getting nearer. Simon saw out of the corner of his eye something that looked like a scorpion scuttling in-between them and the ticket seller. It was larger than the scorpions he'd seen before. But how could it be here? There were no scorpions in England, surely?

The ticket seller saw an enormous insect appear in front of him. He slowed his steps. What on earth was it? He'd read about terrible creatures coming in from Africa in bunches of bananas and plant pots. God, it was getting bigger!

He felt a hand on his shoulder and looked up into the face of a black-suited man. The Knight of the Swan gripped him.

'Are you all right, sir?' he said, calmly.

'The – there – there's a . . . a . . .' the ticket seller pointed helplessly.

The knight looked in the direction of his pointing. 'There's nothing there,' he said.

The ticket seller rubbed his eyes. Of course there was nothing there.

'I know those kids,' said Mark. 'I need to talk to them. I'm from the police.'

'I knew it,' said the ticket seller. 'You lot! Wait a second!'

'We've got to go!' said Flora.

Pike sensed things around them moving and shuddering. He saw shadows stretching from Mark towards them, across the ground, reaching out their tendrils. He gulped and grabbed Flora and Simon by the elbows. He watched as the shadow crept forwards

over a line of ants. He gaped in astonishment. When the shadow had crossed there was a gap in the column, as if the ants it had touched had never been there. He gulped again. 'Flora . . . Simon . . . we've got to go . . .'

The ticket seller and the Knight of the Swan were talking. Then, with one resolve, they turned and headed towards the three.

'I've got the police here!' shouted the ticket seller.

'Bugger,' said Simon. 'What do we do?'

Simon stepped off the kerb, and was pulled back by Flora.

'Don't do that – you'll kill yourselves!' called the seller. 'You just stay where you are!'

The game was up, Simon thought. There was no way they could cross the road.

Pike pointed at the shadows reaching out towards them. 'Don't let them get near you,' he whispered. He pushed them away along the pavement, away from the encroaching darkness. He could see the knight, and as if underneath his form he could see something else that made him shudder, something tight and wrapped up and white.

Simon was about to ask Pike what he meant when there was a screeching of tyres and his attention

was grabbed by the arrival of the snazziest racing green open-topped sports car he'd ever seen. It looked old. It drew up in front of them, its engine throbbing, puffing little bomblets of exhaust into the air. Inside it was a raven-haired woman, and next to her a younger man with reddish-blond hair. On his lap was a spaniel which was barking loudly. The radio was playing some fearsome guitar music. In the back was another young man, almost identical to the one in the front, with a similar haircut. Both were wearing white T-shirts decorated with orange flames, although one set of flames pointed up, and the other pointed down.

The woman looked at the three of them. 'Need a lift?' she said.

Flora blinked. The ticket seller and the knight were now twenty feet away.

Pike was trembling like a frightened puppy, the shadows were inching towards them, extending their tendrils like smoke. *Can't Simon and Flora see them?* he wondered. He pushed the two back again.

'Who are you?' shouted Flora.

'Raven and the Flames,' said the woman. 'Isn't that obvious?'

'Oh yeah, of course,' said Simon.

'You rescued us, after all.'

Then Simon recognised them – the golden people from the tree. Here they were, apparently in fully human form.

'Hey! You!' shouted the ticket seller.

Sir Mark was striding towards them calmly, his face unperturbed. But when he saw the car and its occupants, he stopped in his tracks. His face remained immobile. Pike saw the shadows waver.

A car swerved around Raven's. She didn't appear to notice.

'It's them!' said Pike. 'The ones from the tree . . . Let's go with them.' He put his hand out to the car door.

'How do we know for sure?' said Flora. They did look familiar, but these guys were absolutely human. The ones in the holding place had looked – well, alien.

'Wait!' shouted the seller.

Mark, however, had halted.

'Do we have another option?' said Simon under his breath to Flora.

'They could be agents – friends of the knight!'

'They could be helpers, too, remember?'

'Out of the frying pan into the flames?' said Flora.

'Listen,' said Raven, bringing the clutch up to biting point. 'You getting in or what?'

The ticket seller was now a short distance away.

Without another word Simon slung his rucksack over and squeezed up next to the man in the back; Pike dived in like a ferret after a rabbit, and Flora, a little more demurely, scrambled over.

Just as the ticket seller reached the pavement the car pulled away. He bent over, hands on his knees, panting; then turned to comment sarcastically to his companion. But the man who'd called himself a policeman had gone, as if he had been nothing but shadows and had simply melted away.

'Hah!' Simon couldn't help releasing a yell of triumph, which Flora joined in with. Then, remembering that they knew nothing about their rescuers, he subsided, leaving Flora's whoop to waver out on its own.

'So who are you exactly?' he said as they came out into a country lane that hadn't seen such speed for a long time. Rabbits scattered, birds fled telephone wires and an old lady tending her petunias turned to see a garden gnome wobbling on its base. She caught it just before it fell.

'Yes,' said Flora. 'We need to get somewhere. If

you could just drop us off at the nearest –'

'Well, maybe we should be asking who exactly you are?' interrupted the man in the back, a little too sinisterly for Simon's liking.

Simon, Flora and Pike all felt fear grip their throats. They'd been idiots. Out of the frying pan and into the flames indeed. Flora had been right. Now there was no avenue of escape. An emptiness opened in Simon's mind, wide and deserted, and he saw himself as a tiny figure bounded by nothingness.

'Don't worry. We know who you are. That's how we found you,' said the other man. 'We told you already – you rescued us!'

'But it's OK,' said Raven, overtaking a car much more recklessly than Simon's mother ever had. 'We're here to help you. We were trapped in that holding place, prisoners of the Broken King. So, thanks for rescuing us and everything.'

Simon remembered the little points of light, the strange imprints in the air. 'Weren't there more of you?'

The spaniel turned to look at Simon and yawned.

'We're friends of . . . the messengers. That's what you call them, isn't it? We're not really meant to do much, but – well, it looked difficult back there.'

'Oh good,' said Flora under her breath.

The spaniel barked again, but more happily this time. The two men — although, as Simon looked more closely at them, he realised that they weren't that much older than he was — introduced themselves.

'My name's Cat,' said the one in the front.

'*My* name's Cat,' said the one in the back.

There was something a little feline about them, thought Simon, with their tawny hair, arch expressions and sleepy eyes.

'Are you brothers?' asked Flora.

'No,' they said together.

The dog barked again as they slowed to overtake a horse and rider, who didn't seem that bothered at seeing such a strange collection of people whizz by them.

Raven laughed. 'One's my guitarist. That's Cat in the front. The other's my drummer. That's — well, you can guess. We're a band! Here, at least, we are,' she finished cryptically. 'It's what we choose to be ... We play to our king, at home in the Realm. And here we like to play your music. It's different from ours. Things have changed a bit since we were last here, though.'

'When was that?' asked Simon.

'Well,' said Raven, thinking a bit. 'Time . . . time is a bit . . . when it comes to going between the worlds. I think that it was in what you call the 1970s when we were actually here.'

That explains the car, thought Simon. And then he thought, *Whoa*. 'So when we . . . go to the Broken Kingdom, how much time will have passed when we come back?'

'That way round, less than the time that's spent up here. But we don't quite know how much. It seems to change.'

Simon let the thought roll around his head for a minute, then listened to Raven as she took up her story. 'We were passing through on our way to the Broken Kingdom. We were part of the embassy, the last one . . . We were captured and imprisoned.'

Raven and the Flames, thought Simon. *Good name*. He remembered what the messengers had said about birds and fire. Maybe this was the help they'd mentioned. There'd been something else too. *Birds, fire, gold*.

'How do you . . . I'm sorry,' said Simon, 'but how do I tell you apart?'

'He's nicer than me,' said Cat in the front, and the other man laughed.

'Look at our shirts,' said the Cat in the back. 'I go down.'

'And I go up,' said the Cat in the front.

'Although sometimes we change round. You know, just for kicks.'

'Ignore them,' said Raven as she swung out on to the slip road leading to a motorway. 'Oh, and you'd better put some seatbelts on. Where was it you wanted to go again?'

There wasn't quite enough room in the back for four of them. Simon and Pike shared a seatbelt. It put Simon into quite close contact with Pike's pungency. He couldn't help wrinkling his nose, but tried not to show it.

Pike didn't notice. He was dreamily elsewhere, seeing the shadows stretching along the pavement. The expression on the knight's face.

'London,' said Simon guardedly. He didn't know exactly where – Flora had worked out the map. He was beginning to wonder if accepting the lift had been such a good idea. Who were these crazy people? Were they any less dangerous than the Knight of the Swan? He whispered to Flora. 'Look, shouldn't we just say thank you and get them to drop us off at the next station?'

Flora, however, had changed her mind. 'And then what? We hardly have any money, remember? We'll need as much as we can for the future. We don't know what we're getting into.'

'Don't trust us?' said Cat in the back.

The guitar music pounded. Cat in the front played an imaginary guitar solo and Simon guessed that they were listening to Raven and the Flames in action. There was a heavy bass and frantic drums, and what he supposed was Raven wailing over the top. Despite himself, he quite liked it.

'Not . . . not really,' said Simon.

'You?' said Cat, pointing to Flora and Pike.

Flora, rubbing her finger along the inside of her brother's jacket. 'I don't really,' she said. 'But – thanks for the lift and everything.' Pike said nothing at all.

'We know what you're looking for. Your siblings have disappeared. They've been taken by the Broken King, and now you need to get them back. So you've eaten the shadow. You've faced up to yourselves. You've got disguise,' said Raven.

'Now you need a weapon. You have to steal the sun,' said Cat in the back.

'How do you know that?' said Simon.

'*Everybody* knows that,' scoffed Cat in the back.

'What does it mean?' asked Flora. '*Steal the sun?* It doesn't mean . . . I mean, how could it?' She thought about eating the shadow. That had been about coming to terms with herself, with the shadow inside her. That power seemed to give them the ability to become invisible. *No need to be noticed, any more*, she thought.

'Wait,' said Simon. 'Why did the Knight of the Swan stop when he saw you?'

'What's in your pocket?' said Cat in the front.

With all the running, Simon had forgotten. He left the question about the Knight of the Swan for later.

He'd meant to look at the little creature earlier, but hadn't wanted to in front of Flora and Pike. Now he supposed he had to. But how did the Cat know?

Blushing slightly at his concealment, he pulled the tiny bird-deer from his jeans.

He'd already named it – Hover. It lay inert in his hand.

'Thought I could sense something,' said the Cat in the back, and held out his hand. 'That's from the Golden Realm. It's been sent to you by the messengers.'

Simon retracted his palm, but Cat smiled, took

Simon's hand gently and opened it. Then he bent slightly and breathed on the tiny creature – and Simon saw that his breath was like a sunbeam. Pike's head switched round and his gaze locked on to what was happening.

The miniature bird-deer shivered and rustled its wings. They shimmered in the light, their many colours making a rainbow as it fluttered. Hover trotted around, looking inquisitively upwards, then flitted on to Cat's shoulder, nuzzling his neck with its tiny nose. Cat in the back beamed and let it clamber down his arm and on to his hand, as if it were a pet lizard or mouse.

'Where did you get that?' said Flora.

Simon sensed her envy. 'I was going to tell you . . . but . . .'

Cat in the back said, 'The messengers gave it to you, didn't they?'

Simon nodded. 'Well, they didn't physically give it to me . . . but after the shadowsnake, I . . . felt it arrive.'

'Why didn't you tell me?' said Flora.

'I didn't know what it was!' answered Simon. The air washed through his hair.

Flora crossed her arms as Pike leaned forwards

eagerly to look at the little creature as it pranced about in the cradle of Cat's hands.

'It's so you can tell who's on your side. Only we can make it come alive – that is, only beings from the Golden Realm. It'll react to people who are friendly to you here as well. The Knight of the Swan wouldn't be able to do this – nor would anyone on his side.'

Simon didn't like all this talk about sides. He remembered the messengers' hesitancy earlier about their ability to enter the world where Anna and Johnny were being kept . . . prisoner or hostage? The messengers hadn't really explained. Were they coming into some sort of a dispute, some terrible battle between worlds they'd never heard of, could never dream of? He thought back to when he'd left his parents' house. The last normal thing he remembered doing was drinking a cup of tea. He wondered if he'd ever do the same again.

As the hills flashed by them, the little bird-deer cantered around happily on Cat in the back's open palm, and Simon reached out to stroke it. It came to his finger. He felt not solidity exactly, but a resistance that seemed welcoming.

'Is it alive?' asked Flora.

'Not really,' said Cat in the back. 'It's more a

collection of energy. They might have sent it to you for something else, though, as well. I can't think what for the moment.'

Cat in the back said, 'But we should get down to business. We know where the sunsword is.'

'They don't know what that is,' said Raven. Shouting into the slipstream, she continued, 'It's a weapon made out of flame. The Broken King hid it – it used to belong to us. You'll need it to get to his world. And another one – of us – is trapped there. If you succeed, you will release him too.' She looked serious for a moment.

'So you know where he hid it?'

'Yep,' said the Cats at the same time.

'So we can get it easily?'

'Nope,' said the Cats.

'Ah,' said Simon, reaching over to scratch the chin of the spaniel. Nothing, he reflected, was ever that easy.

'But we can point you in the right direction.'

'Good,' said Simon. 'And thank you.'

'No problem.'

As they drove, Simon studied the little bird-deer, which had now curled up in the crook between his thumb and first finger. He saw Flora's profile, the

wind blowing her hair over her face, and he saw Pike staring into the far distance. He remembered his parents, and he thought of them lying in some golden sleep, unaware of what was happening, unaware of the darkness that seemed to lie everywhere.

They sped towards London. The others kept quiet. It wasn't till they reached Dorking that Raven said, 'Right. First things first. You don't have much time. So let's head to our gig.'

'How did you manage that?' said Flora.

'We are persuasive when we want to be,' said one of the Cats, winking.

Flora, against her better judgement, felt a bit flustered.

'Well . . . I guess,' said Simon, and Raven pressed down the accelerator as they zoomed into the afternoon, towards the sunsword. The dog sat up and put his face into the breeze, and Simon and Flora lifted their hands into the air, feeling the wind. Pike's hands were folded in his lap and his face looked down at his feet. He was still thinking about shadows.

As they entered the southern suburbs of London, Simon remembered how he and his family had left the city a year ago, most of their possessions sold or reclaimed, and the tiny hired car they'd used to drive

out down to the south coast. He remembered how he'd run from the cottage . . . how long ago now? Was it yesterday, or the day before? He wasn't clear. Raven was right about time. How long had they spent in that holding place? He couldn't tell.

Soon they had slipped into some quiet streets around the British Museum. Flora was enjoying herself – she loved London and couldn't help but get excited about it, even if they were entering unknown territory. The two Cats spoke and acted a bit like her brother Johnny. She liked them, with their blond and gunmetal hair and their supercilious smiles. She'd gone to concerts once or twice with Johnny, when he hadn't been drunk or high, and they'd been some of the happiest moments of her life.

Pike had retreated into himself – if at all possible, more than before. The piercing vision that had come to him as he entered that strange holding place was troubling him greatly, but he had no means to describe it to Flora and Simon. Now that he'd seen them in that empty way he felt too connected to them, though he dreamed of leaving too. He knew something that they didn't know – something vast and terrible and dark – but he could not break it down into words. That cart, bearing its awful burden

through the darkening streets, that tall and hooded figure, the empty eyes of his friends . . .

Raven and the two Cats slid out of the car like rock stars. Laughing, Flora and Simon followed them. Raven looked at her watch. 'We haven't actually got much time,' she said. 'They'll be on to us now.' She swore quietly under her breath. 'We've arranged a small concert in a club. We're on about nine thirty.'

She was unlocking the door to a block of flats into which the two Cats piled, followed by the spaniel and the three friends.

'You live here?' said Simon. 'Or . . . lived here?' It was one room, without any decoration and just one sofa. Simon wasn't sure but he thought he saw a scorpion again, calmly sitting in the shadows. It seemed quite friendly, as scorpions go, but Simon decided not to say anything about it. It might, after all, be a figment of his imagination.

He needn't have worried, because Pike had seen it too, although he also kept it to himself. For him it was one more troubling sign amongst everything else that had thrown itself at him in the past few days.

Flora hadn't seen it. She was too busy enjoying the Cats looking at her.

'Well, sort of,' said Raven. 'You see, whether we're

actually *here* or not is another matter.'

'I might have guessed,' said Flora, wondering if it was all right to fancy someone that wasn't strictly a human, even if they were in the shape of one. The Cat she was looking at blew her a kiss, then pretended to catch one she'd thrown back, though she hadn't.

'Map?' said Raven.

'Map? Oh yes,' said Simon, and they took it out from its hiding place and unrolled it on the floor, which was the only place they could unroll it, given the general lack of tables. He felt the unease he always felt when opening it, as if it were a living creature.

'There, you see the dot there?' said Raven. 'You'll have worked out by now that the map changes to show whatever you're looking for. That's where the sunsword is. The Broken King hid it – he has a sense of humour sometimes – in the Temple of Mithras. That's on Walbrook Street.'

'I thought it was near here,' said Flora. 'I'm sure I've been on a trip to see it.'

'Mithras?' said Pike. Everyone turned to look at him. He said it again. He liked the sound of the syllables, dark and rolling in his mouth, like berries, like chocolate.

'He's what you call a demi-god, associated with

the sun,' said one of the Cats. 'So we know all about him, obviously.'

'Obviously,' said Flora uncertainly.

'The Romans worshipped him. We are his friends – his companions. We've been separated from him since we were trapped.'

A thought occurred to Simon. *Why* had they been trapped? He was about to say something when Raven continued.

'So the plan is for us to all go to the concert as if nothing else is happening, then we'll make a sort of diversion whilst you head off to the temple. You'll have to use the shadow.'

'And how do we steal the sun exactly?' asked Simon.

Raven and the Cats looked at each other. 'It used to be a ceremonial thing. The ambassador of our realm would carry the sunsword on his visits to the Broken Kingdom – before it was broken, of course. Our last ambassador –'

'On the day of the first Taking Apart,' added one of the Cats.

'– he was also taken apart, and the sunsword was stolen and hidden at the same time as we were entrapped with the shadows. Now you'll need it.'

'What for?' asked Flora. The shadow – that was disguise. That seemed easy enough to understand – they could get into the Kingdom without anyone noticing. But a sword? She'd never used a sword before – still less any weapon, apart from doing a bit of archery, and that hadn't involved getting anywhere near the target.

'You'll see,' said Raven grimly. 'So you can use this place whenever you like. Now, let's get going. Our stuff's already there.'

Just before they left, she paused, and turned to them. 'Now listen,' she said. 'What you're about to face is dangerous, but I know you can do this. And a lot rests on it – more than you can know, for the moment. Just remember – your siblings are out there and they're trapped and they need you. OK?'

They muttered agreement and went outside. On the pavement it was warm. The green car sat purring like a cricket. The two Cats were first in, bickering between themselves over a biscuit. Raven leaped into the front and gunned the engine.

Well, thought Simon. *Here goes nothing.*

Chapter Ten

THE TEMPLE
OF MITHRAS

THE DOORMAN IN front of the nightclub where Raven and the Flames were playing raised an eyebrow as Flora, Simon and Pike came to the door. They were all wearing sunglasses to make them look older – Raven had pressed a pair each on Pike and Flora – but a quick nod from Raven stopped the bouncer from questioning them.

'Have a good night,' he muttered as he grudgingly stepped aside to let them in.

Simon and the others went down some steep steps into a basement pounding with music. Simon had never been to a nightclub before and was nervous.

He gulped as a man in a leather jacket pushed past him, and dived for the safety of the bar.

Pike had never been to one either and looked at all the people around him. *Great*, he thought. *I can hide here. Nobody will notice me. They're all too busy looking at each other.*

'What are you doing?' called Flora, who had been to nightclubs before with Johnny. 'Come and dance!' *That's what Anna said to me*, thought Simon, *before I called the Broken King*. He faltered.

Flora was about to go out into the centre of the empty dance floor when Raven caught her by the sleeve.

'OK, guys,' said Raven. 'What did I say about being careful? Go to the bar, have a drink on us.'

Flora made a sound of disappointment and Simon couldn't help smiling. Pike ducked behind a pillar.

'Cranberry juice,' said one of the Cats, not that Simon had really thought of ordering much else.

'Make that four,' Simon said to the barman, who'd appeared and was looking at them with interest. Flora, Simon and Pike sat down carefully on red barstools, and swivelled towards each other.

Simon thought of being watched. Raven had told

them to use the shadow when they left. It would buy them time until they got to the Temple of Mithras on Walbrook Street.

He looked around in the dingy room. Any of these people might be an agent. He thought of the Knight of the Swan. The hideous shadowsnake. The dark beast that had first attacked them. The messenger had called it a royal hound.

He thought about how he'd obeyed the messengers. He thought about how, buried deep under his need to find Anna, was the thought of his own oblivion. He shuddered and took a sip of his cranberry juice.

Pike pulled his sleeve, and he looked up to see that Flora was sliding down her stool, desperate to get up and dance. One of the Cats came along and took Pike by the shoulder in a friendly grip, pushing him away from the other two.

'I just can't help it,' said Flora, in reply to Simon's questioning face.

Raven stepped in between them and Pike. She cut in tersely. 'Now. There aren't as many agents of the Broken King as before, and they're behaving . . . strangely. The Broken King knows who you are, knows what you want, and he doesn't want you to get your siblings back.'

'Why?' asked Flora, sitting back fully on her stool.

Raven looked away. 'It's . . . a contract. He has a mind that is very . . . Well, it used to be precise. Now, there's a reason he's the Broken King. Some say he's gone mad, that the Kingdom is in turmoil . . .' She paused. 'But that shouldn't worry you. He calls the children he takes the Blessed Ones.'

'Why? What does he want them for?' Simon said. Lights flashed across the room as he finished his cranberry juice. Cat leaned in further to Pike, talking companionably. Pike looked entranced.

'We don't know. Our spies are few and they risk their lives every day . . .'

Spies? thought Simon.

Raven noticed that he was about to ask another question and changed the subject quickly. 'You remember the way to Walbrook Street?'

Simon nodded. They'd explained the points on the map to him and Flora, but he'd memorised it anyway. Raven had been quite insistent that Pike not go with them, which Simon found a little strange, but he'd put it out of his mind.

'We've prepared a little something to cause confusion,' said one of the Cats. 'You just go like

we talked about. When you see yourselves on stage. That's the signal.'

'OK,' said Simon slowly.

The thrashing music of the band onstage rose to a climax. The singer yelled and threw himself down on to the floor. Everybody cheered.

'See ourselves ... on stage...' Simon remembered back to the shadow versions of himself and Flora in that strange holding place where they'd eaten the shadow. But he knew that this wouldn't be like that. The powers coming from Raven and her friends were too warm, too kindly. 'Make sure Pike doesn't see you,' she said. 'Go now and wait by the entrance.'

It looked like Cat was telling Pike a joke; Pike was laughing, at any rate. Simon and Flora slipped off their stools and made their way through the gathering crowds to the door. Cat released Pike, and motioned to him.

Simon watched Raven and the two Cats slip backstage, Pike following them. The band clasped hands with various people – a woman with purple dreadlocks, a man with piercings in his chin and eyebrows.

Despite himself, Simon was excited. Unlike Flora,

who was jumping into gig mode like a dolphin through a hoop, Simon had never been to one before and wasn't sure what to expect.

The lights went low. Then Raven and the Flames burst on to the stage. Their shadows seemed to make a scorpion on the wall. Simon thought he saw the spaniel sitting by the drums, but the dog seemed bigger, more menacing. The music thrummed through the air. The girl with purple dreadlocks shook violently. Flora's foot tapped. Simon kept an eye out for anything that might be an enemy agent, but he couldn't see anyone that might be one. He fervently hoped that the Knight of the Swan was nowhere nearby. The Knight of the Swan – it sounded so lovely, but Simon bet that it hid ugliness, just as a graceful swan is kept moving by its thick paddling feet.

'I'd like to welcome some special guests tonight,' shouted Raven into the microphone, causing feedback to bounce off the walls. 'They're a young band, and they're going to provide some extra vocals and guitar for us today. It's The Wanderers!'

Flora and Simon were immensely surprised to see themselves walk on to the stage – only it wasn't really themselves. This Flora and Simon seemed to

emanate light, although of course it may only have been a trick of the stage lighting.

It was the signal. Simon and Flora thought back to eating the shadow. Simon wondered if it would be as painful again. He opened the black sphere. There were four little balls left. He quietly ate one and watched Flora do the same.

They didn't have much time. Raven had said that their copies would last about an hour. They slipped out of the club and into the street. Pike came out from backstage just after they left and settled in happily to watch the show.

Outside it was still light, and the brightness was a little dizzying after the darkness of the club but Simon and Flora soon got used to it. They ran, Simon holding Flora's hand, past office workers, through the cream and white streets around the Bank of England. They came to the end of Walbrook Street and slid down a little alleyway where a Georgian house sat beneath the wings of a glass and steel office building. Simon and Flora halted by a church.

This was exactly where the map told them that the sunsword would be. There was a tiny door in the side of the church, which looked far too small to be a proper door. A young man with blond curly hair

came out of the church. He looked directly at them.

'Surely he can't see us?' whispered Simon to Flora.

'Probably one of the curates or something,' said Flora, whose knowledge of the church hierarchy was relatively limited.

'Guess this is it,' said Simon. Just to be sure, when the curly-haired young man looked away, Simon pushed the handle of the door. It gave a little resistance, but opened sure enough.

Both Simon and Flora had to stoop to get through it. It opened on to a crypt.

'Oh,' said Simon.

'I can't see anything here . . .' said Flora. 'No door or anything.'

They backed out. Simon closed the door again and thought. 'The button.' He fished it out of his pocket. 'Might as well try.' He felt around the door, but couldn't find anything to fit it in.

'What about the pencil?'

Simon shrugged and pulled it out too. He looked at it for a second, then fitted it into the keyhole and jiggled it around.

Something clicked. Simon arched his eyebrows at Flora, and pushed open the door once more.

Simon gasped. They heard immediately the trickle

of water and they saw not the crypt of a church, but a stream. 'The Walbrook,' Simon whispered.

'But I thought it was concreted over?'

'I guess we must be in another layer of reality. Like where the shadows were, in that holding place. Like where my . . .' He was about to say like where his parents were, but bit his tongue. 'It feels different from . . . that other place.' He didn't want to talk about the shadowsnake, in case even evoking the name brought it back.

'Look,' hissed Flora. By the entrance to the door was a group of life-sized stone statues. There was a young man straddling a bull, killing it with a sword that seemed like it gleamed with real bronze. The young man was looking upwards in ecstasy. On either side of him stood two youths, one holding a flaming torch pointing upwards, the other pointing down. A bird perched on a ledge behind. There was a scorpion, larger than life, whilst a dog sat by the man's feet, and at the other side of the stone grouping there was a snake sliding out of the wall.

'There's an inscription,' said Flora. 'It's in Latin. I think.'

'What does it say?'

'Well, there are two names.' She spelled them out

with difficulty. 'Cautes and Cautopates. That's the two torchbearers.'

'The way you say it, sounds like . . .'

'Two cats?'

'And I'm guessing that bird is . . .'

'A raven,' said Flora.

'So Raven and the Flames . . .'

'Yes,' said Flora.

'So who's the dude?'

'That must be Mithras himself.'

'And the snake?'

Flora shrugged.

Simon closed the door behind him. They followed the stream, which ran sluggishly. Though they appeared to be underground, in some kind of tunnel, with no sign of a moon or stars above them, there was light from somewhere, almost like daylight. *Is the light coming from the rocks themselves?* thought Simon.

They also seemed to be going down a slope. Simon could not see very far to the left or right. He reached out with his hands and couldn't feel anything on either side of him.

They followed the stream. Suddenly Simon felt some air on his face, and in the dim light he saw that it was flowing into what must be a large cave. Simon

held Flora back from walking straight over the edge of the rock into the stream. They stood, poised, on the edge of it.

The stream went into the cave, apparently splitting it in two. Simon could make out small clusters of things on the ground – white stones, he thought.

Simon shouted, experimentally, and his voice came echoing back to him. *It must be quite large,* he thought. On the other side of the stream was a ledge, and behind it what looked like an opening into a further cave. The light gleamed silver off the rocks. Moisture dripped down from above, cold on to Simon's nose.

'On the ledge,' said Simon, and pointed.

There was something hanging down, held by wires he couldn't see, or at least that's what Simon assumed. He put a foot tentatively into the stream, and started to wade across. It was maybe ten paces across, he thought, and not that deep. In the middle it only came up to his shins. He reached the rocky shore on the side where the thing hung.

'Be careful!' said Flora.

Simon paced forwards warily trying not to think about what might be lurking in the darkness. The thing was glowing brightly. As he came closer, he

saw that it was a scabbard, with the hilt of a sword poking out of the end of it.

'This must be it,' he whispered over his shoulder. His whispers rushed around the cave, reverberating everywhere.

'Grab it and let's get out of here!' hissed Flora. Her voice joined his, echoing and strange.

What about the guardian? thought Simon. *I hope it sleeps deeply, whatever it is . . .*

'Hurry!' said Flora.

This might be the easiest task yet, thought Simon. *That's not what usually happens.* He licked his dry lips and prepared himself. *It's almost within reach. I just have to hold out my hand and take it.* He took a deep breath, then without stopping to think any further, he grabbed the scabbard with his right hand.

A drop of water fell on to his nose. He wiped it off with his other hand. 'I've got it!' he couldn't help saying. He heard Flora moving behind him, and readied himself. The scabbard was warm to touch, and he took it easily with his other hand and pulled it away from the blade.

It came away easily, lightly even. He held sword and scabbard above his head in triumph, then resheathed the sword.

Then he felt the shadow leaving him and the sound of steps behind him. He turned and saw a girl standing on the edge of the stream, the same side as he was. *Where did she come from?* thought Simon. *Deeper in . . . that cave . . .* She looked about Flora's age, Simon thought, maybe a couple of years older. She was silvery and pale and calm. Extremely calm. She said nothing, but bowed, very slightly.

'That's the guardian?' whispered Flora from the other side. 'Wow, I could take her out. She can't see us, anyway. Can she?'

The girl was holding a sword, and hiding something behind her back. She grinned and brought it out into the open. It was a helmet of gleaming silver in the shape of a lion's head. She put the helmet on. Then she pawed at the ground, raised her head, and leaped towards them with her sword held high.

'Oh,' said Flora. 'She can see us.'

The girl headed straight for Simon, like an arrow from a bow, roaring. She stormed at Simon and swiped at him with her sword, knocking the sunsword out of his grip and into a dark corner. Simon leaped back into the stream, splashing through the cold,

and joined Flora, panting, on the other side.

'Now what?' said Simon out of the corner of his mouth.

The guardian snorted, a real animal snort, and Simon and Flora were horrified to see that the lion mask was animated, had become part of her skin and was now to all intents and purposes her face.

Simon saw death in those eyes. He saw countless mauled victims. He saw himself and Flora bleeding to death amongst the piles of things on the ground that now he saw were piles of bones.

Before them flowed the sluggish, cool waters; behind the waters the girl paced and roared; behind her Simon and Flora could see the radiance of the sunsword shining in the shadows.

As Simon and Flora faced down the guardian of the sunsword, Pike sat in the club watching their decoys onstage. He felt suddenly as he had done in the holding place, when he'd had the vision. The room around him, already flashing with different coloured lights and movement, began to pulse in and out of reality and was replaced with scenes that, as in dreams, seemed both familiar and unfamiliar. One second he was sitting between a man in black

leathers and another in a purple T-shirt; the next he was . . . elsewhere.

He could feel a pathway forming in front of himself, one down which he, Flora and Simon ought not to go. There was a moment, a turn, where the possibility of what he saw would become a reality. Where Flora and Simon sat on a cart, drawn by a strange beast. And he, Pike – where was he?

He couldn't work it out. He didn't have that feeling in dreams where you are both agent and watcher; he didn't have that at all. He could see many people milling about the cart and the hooded figure driving it. He could hear wailing and soft, strange music. He knew that if Simon and Flora met that hooded figure, it would be the end of them. He had to tell them, and he had to tell them now. But they were up there, singing and playing. He sat impatiently, fingering the sleeves of his top.

Fear had descended on Simon. He was weaponless, trapped and facing a being that would certainly kill him – and Flora too. He scanned about, but could see nothing that might help him.

The guardian pawed the ground again and snarled, revealing a row of sharp, pointed silver teeth. She was

pacing now from side to side, assessing the situation.

Simon thought furiously. They were in a temple to a demi-god associated with the sun . . . He remembered the stone statues at the entrance to the tunnel. The god Mithras was wielding a bronze sword. *Maybe I can use that sword,* he thought.

He heard the long, heavy breathing of the guardian and smelled a foul sweat coming off her.

It was their only option. *We can't overcome her with bones,* thought Simon.

'Mithras's sword,' Simon said to Flora, under his breath. 'I'll distract her, you go get it.' He leaned down to pick up some pebbles from the bank. 'When I throw, run!'

Simon hurled a stone at the guardian and it pinged off her helmet. He yelled and ran towards her, volleying with the stones. At the same time, Flora sprinted back towards the entrance of the tunnel.

Simon ran off in the other direction. 'You'd better yield!' he shouted. 'You don't want to get in my way!'

The guardian, snorting with laughter, strode after him, facing Simon from the other side of the bank, her sword outstretched.

If only I can keep her busy, thought Simon, *and outpace her.*

He plunged into the stream and made it to the other side. He stood there, panting and jumping from one foot to the other.

'Come and fight me!' he called.

The guardian ran towards him. Simon waded back across, the guardian hard on his heels. Simon ran further down the bank until he was facing the ledge where he could see the sunsword shining in the corner.

The guardian reached the bank on his side, wading with some difficulty. *She's weighed down by that helmet,* thought Simon. *Good.* As soon as she came on to dry land, Simon plunged back into the water and splashed across, heading straight for the sunsword. 'Can't catch me!' he yelled, knowing full well that she could.

Meanwhile, Flora had reached the stone statues at the entrance. She could see Mithras with his sword out. From far away she could hear Simon taunting the guardian and the guardian roaring back, and the two of them splashing in the river, and she could feel cold air swirling round her and the darkness shivering with movement. *Here goes nothing,* she thought, and grabbed the sword of Mithras with both hands.

Immediately a shadow coiled out from the wall and branched around her wrist. She plucked at it and

managed to throw it off, in just enough time to grab the hilt of the sword again.

But the shadow sprang back, only now it grabbed her round the neck and started choking her. With one hand Flora scrabbled at the shadow, trying to get it off her; with the other she yanked at the hilt of the sword. She could hardly breath.

Simon was on the ledge where the sunsword had hung. The sunsword's radiance made it warm.

The guardian had crossed the river and was facing him. The sunsword was behind him. The guardian's eyes were reddish and dull, replaced with an entirely mechanical fury. She charged at him. Now she seemed far more lion than girl. Her teeth shone savagely. Simon dodged out of the way, but the edge of her sword caught him on the upper part of his right arm, and he let out a cry of pain. Lashing out, he grabbed the guardian and with inspired force thrust her to the ground.

She bucked ferociously underneath him, then lay still. Simon held down the top of her chest and put his other hand on the top of her head. The helmet felt like skin, like fur. Those red eyes gazed at him, as if laughing, as if asking how a little boy could really hold her down. She wasn't even trying to get up. And

sure enough, with the barest flick of her body, she sent Simon hurtling into the wall of the cave.

His arm throbbing, Simon lay there, his entire body lit with pain. The guardian seemed to have grown larger, her snarl to have become more wicked. The sunsword was out of his reach.

The guardian leaned over him. One toss of her head and he was doomed, done for, his parents childless. She tilted her head to the left and roared a savage roar, ready to gore him through and through with her sword. And there was nothing Simon could do.

Raven and the Flames had come to their last song. Pike, not waiting for Simon and Flora to come off, had gone backstage. He grabbed them as they came down the stairs, glowing with exertion.

'I have to tell you,' he said.

They looked at him blankly.

'I've got to tell you. You can't trust him. The man in the hood. I know if you meet him that will be it. You'll be . . . empty. That's all I know. Listen to me!'

Still smiling vacantly, the decoy Simon and Flora went past him to the bar, leaving Pike even more frustrated than before.

* * *

Simon saw the heavy head tilt towards him. He wondered what death would be like. *I don't accept death*, he thought. *I don't. This is not the time.* He wondered if he could roll over and escape. No, he couldn't – he would only expose his softer flank. He kicked out at the girl with all the force he could. She reared for one final thrust. Simon tensed.

The guardian groaned and shifted. Behind her Simon could make out Flora's head, her face set into grim determination. She whacked the bronze sword at the guardian, knocking her backwards a pace or two.

'Thanks,' said Simon frantically, as he clambered upwards.

Flora was watching the guardian.

Simon leaped to the sunsword. He grabbed it – its hilt warm to the touch.

The guardian moaned. Simon unsheathed the sword. It was long, silver and gold at the same time. He was almost blown back by the heat coming off it.

'Quick, Simon!' Flora was clashing with the guardian again, her bronze sword now not seeming much of a defence against the guardian's might.

Simon went to swing, then hesitated. 'She's only a girl!'

The guardian went for Flora, who just managed to ward her off.

'Take her helmet off!' shouted Simon.

'And how exactly am I meant to do that?' yelled Flora as she smashed the guardian on the side of her face.

'Knock her out!'

Taking advantage of the guardian's momentary instability, Flora stepped in again and knocked her round the other side of the face.

The guardian faltered, rocked and fell. Immediately, as she lay on the ground, she seemed to shrink again. The animated face started to look more like something made out of silver.

At the same time Flora said, 'Do it!'

'I can't!' Simon said.

And then they heard another voice, calm and awesome, and a shining figure emerged from the deeper cave.

For some reason there was no need for him to say anything. Light gleamed off his golden hair and he emanated peaceful, golden light. He was tall and handsome, and he wore a long, flowing robe that was embroidered with symbols of the sun.

Flora and Simon both paused and turned to

stare at him. Simon suddenly felt that he shouldn't be doing anything violent in front of this beautiful person. Flora too was awed and stepped back from the guardian. The guardian let out a whimper and seemed to relax, as if she knew it was all over now.

That must be Mithras, thought Simon, his heart beating. *He's been released. Did we do that?* He and Flora both instinctively dropped to their knees and bowed their heads.

'Get up,' said the figure calmly.

He held out his hand and Flora knew what to do. She stood up and walked slowly towards him, and gave him the bronze sword she was holding. It was his sword, after all. The sword of Mithras.

'You have the sunsword,' he said.

Simon showed it to Mithras.

'You are on your way to the Broken Kingdom.'

Simon nodded, unable to form words.

Mithras returned the nod and smiled, his face dazzling, his eyes bright. 'You have done well. Now you don't have much time.' The shining man held his own sword high above his head. The only thing he said further was, 'Go.' In his hands the bronze sword lengthened and glowed and hummed and looked sharp and deathly.

Simon sprang up, and he and Flora fled from the cave – Simon holding the sunsword – down past the brackish river, towards the entrance of the tunnel. They were panting, exhausted. They reached the door, rushed through it, muddied and dirtied, and ran out into the street where it was still light.

The curly-haired young man from the church watched them go.

Back in the cave, when their footsteps had died away, Mithras – the grave, young, shining man – lowered his sword. He said to the guardian, 'That was well done, your highness, and bravely too. I must thank you also for your kindnesses to me in my captivity.'

The guardian took off her helmet, panting, and laid it beside her, and there it was just a helmet and no more.

'You are welcome, Lord Mithras. They must reach the Kingdom,' she said. 'My father ... He grows worse every day. He executed the Black Knight, my lord. The Black Knight – his favourite! The Knight of the Swan is charged to stop these children finding the way ... I have done all I can to help them, but it is becoming harder ... I fear that he begins to suspect me. I fear everyone – their looks, their lying tongues ...'

'You have done well,' said Mithras. 'Once they are there, you will be able to help them further, and when they take their siblings back . . .'

'Then . . . he will lose his power.'

'And you, my princess, will be queen, and will mend the Broken Kingdom.'

The princess looked stony faced. 'Though I have no wish to be so . . .' She swallowed, and looked straight at Mithras. 'Strike me,' she said. 'Strike me, Lord Mithras, so that they will think that I fought well, so that I can say to my lord father the king that the children fought me and defeated me. I will be dishonoured, but I will not be killed.'

Mithras hesitated, then nicked her arm with the tip of his sword. It looked like he'd ripped her, but he was careful. The princess did not make a sound.

The golden man smiled and brought his sword down on the princess's helmet. He sliced it in two, as if it had been nothing more than a piece of meat. From out of the shadows came two more men, and something that looked like a dog, and something that looked like a scorpion. A bird flew from nowhere and landed on his shoulder.

'Say no more,' whispered the princess. 'Say no more.'

Mithras stood over her. The princess pushed

herself up without his help, patted herself down, and bowed to Mithras. The split lion helmet lay to her side. She picked the bits up, ruefully.

'Now we shall part.'

'And if we meet, neither will know each other, nor speak, though it be in peace or on the battlefield,' said the princess, quietly.

'And that we hope not.' Mithras's words were solemn, yet there was a joy around the edges of them that could almost be physically felt.

Once more she bowed, almost touching the ground this time, and Mithras bowed too. And when his head grazed the stone, he was gone, and so were his companions.

The princess turned the parts of the lion helmet round in her hands, once, twice; then she vanished. The halves fell to the rocky ground, and her blood made a dark pool on the stone.

Chapter Eleven

GILES
CUTHBERTSON

'IT'S NOT WORKING.' They were in the tiny flat on their hands and knees, looking at the skin-map. Both Simon and Flora were sucking their fingers from where they'd pricked them with the porcupine spine and the syringe. They'd run back from Walbrook Street and found Pike waiting for them sulkily on the sofa. He'd turned away from them as they'd entered, but Simon and Flora had been too het up to really notice. Raven and the others had come back a short while later.

Flora was clutching the sunsword. She loved its warmth. She felt drawn to it, never wanted to let it

go. In its sheath it looked so harmless, so innocuous, like a walking stick or a furled-up umbrella. But she knew what power it held.

The map lay on the floor. Raven and the two Cats were standing, fidgeting, by the wall with their backs against it, and Pike was sitting on the tiny sofa, his head in his hands, his mind full of a kind of numbness.

The map was blank.

'I don't know what to say,' said Raven unhelpfully.

Simon sat back on his heels. He could feel the miniature bird-deer, pressed against his skin. He wondered where its life-sized counterparts were. He remembered that what he was looking at was Anna's skin, and a pall of sadness fell over him. It was a thick cloak, something that choked and veiled him, something that he knew he would never be able to throw off. *Even when I find her,* he thought.

The Cats were stretching and yawning. Raven looked apologetically at Simon. 'They want to go home,' she said. 'It's hard for us to be here. We were trapped in that place for so long . . . And now that our lord Mithras is free, we can go back – back to our homes . . .'

'So you can't help us?' asked Simon, looking up

from where he'd been studying the floorboards intently.

Raven held out her hands. 'Not any more. The closer we get to the entrance of the Broken Kingdom, the more dangerous it gets for us . . .'

'Why?' said Simon, anger building up. 'Why is it any more dangerous for you than it is for us? We've had to deal with things we didn't even know existed – this is your world, you know more about it than we do! I just want to find Anna . . .'

In the silence after he finished, one of the Cats came to Simon and put his arms around him. Simon felt warmth radiating from him, a comfort that he hadn't experienced for days. A comfort denied to Anna, as well. He found that tears were choking up his eyes. Not wanting to look bad in front of Flora, he forced them to stop. But he stayed with Cat for a few seconds more.

The other Cat spoke in a voice kind but sharp. 'We have to go.'

'You can use this place as a base, whilst you need it,' said Raven as she enveloped Simon and Flora. She then tried to hug Pike, but he remained as still as a statue. She released him without comment. 'You're safe inside,' she continued. 'We've put up

certain wards. Even the Knight of the Swan can't break through them.'

'And when we're outside?'

'Be alert. Always alert.'

'Where are you going?' asked Flora.

'Back,' said Raven. 'Back to . . . our world. We've been talking to them. They speak of you much there. We will watch you. There is more . . .' And once again, she stopped herself. 'Poor children,' she said, and both Simon and Flora were bristling too much at being called children to wonder why she said it. The two of them joined Pike on the sofa. Pike hardly made room for them. He was still upset that neither had made any reference to what he'd told them at the nightclub.

They watched as Raven and the two Cats came together. A glow emanated from their skins – the same sort of glow that came from the bird-deer. It was hot, too, almost searing and tropical. As Simon watched Raven, he saw that she seemed to pulse between forms: she was a woman, then she was bird-like – not a bird, but bird-like, a creature feathered and taloned and with deep black eyes. It was also, thought Simon, old – far older than Raven had been. But he was not afraid.

The Cats did not change shape, but stayed in their almost identical, dandyish forms. From out of the shadows, however, came the spaniel and the scorpion, and they too shimmered between forms, now humanoid, now entirely animal. It all happened very quickly. The warmth increased and Simon felt sweat tickle his forehead, and then there was a flash, a ripping sound, and then there was nothing.

Was there nothing, or was there the shape of a golden snake that curled away? He rubbed his eyes. It must have been an afterglow.

After they'd rested for a while, Simon and Flora set out to the newsagent's on the corner. Pike stayed behind.

Flora loaded up a basket with what food they could find (mostly tins and frozen meat) in case they had to stick around for a while, and they were now walking back. Given the brightness of the day, their sunglasses were not unusual. Many people on the street were in shorts, T-shirts and summer dresses.

Flora and Simon had decided to act in public like brother and sister, to call each other by different names, and generally to keep a very low profile. They were scuttling along the side of the road that was in shadow. No tourist waddling or worker

marching would ever have noticed them, or thought they were unusual in any way.

When they got back, Flora asked Pike to help her make up some kind of lunch (effectively beans on toast), whilst Simon looked through the newspapers.

They discovered, somewhat to their discomfort, that there were no beds in the flat, so they got out the sleeping bag, made pallets of the sofa cushions, and slept in different corners of the room.

Or at least, tried to sleep, as each was woken in the night.

Simon woke up more than the others, seeing fantastical shapes when he did, men bending over him with knives, huge insects beating their wings in the corners of the rooms, only for them to resolve themselves into shadows, and for him to lie, sweating and awake, until dawn.

'We have to do *something*.'

It was the next morning. Flora had already done the washing up and tidied everything away. 'This place gives a whole new meaning to the phrase *cabin fever*.'

'Raven said we shouldn't go out if we didn't have to,' said Simon.

'I'd like to go out,' said Pike unexpectedly.

Flora and Simon tried not to look surprised. 'Oh. OK, then,' said Flora. 'Well. Let's go on a – what do MPs do?'

'Why? We're not MPs,' said Simon.

'Never mind. A fact-finding mission,' said Flora.

'Yes,' said Simon.

'To the British Museum. It's not far from here.'

'Why there?' asked Simon.

'Because we need facts. Hard facts. We've got a map that won't tell us where to go. We've got friends who vanished, quite literally, into thin air. And the only thing we have to go on is that we just took the sunsword from the Temple of Mithras.'

'So?' asked Simon.

'So where do they know about things like the Temple of Mithras? It's not much of a clue, but I remember seeing a statue of him in the British Museum on a school trip. So we should go there, maybe – at least it would get us out of here.'

'And there might be some other information there,' said Simon.

'Genius,' said Flora, not quite sarcastically.

Pike wasn't quite sure what a museum was, so kept his mouth shut. The sound of the word, though,

stirred some memory in him, but he couldn't place it. He had another sudden flash of insight – the cart again, but now the hooded figure was bending over, and the hood was falling away, and the face . . . the face, he felt like he knew that pale face . . . He shook the vision from his mind. *Why haven't they said anything to me about it?* he thought. *They don't seem to be at all interested in it. And I know it's dangerous, I know it'll hurt them. If they aren't listening to me . . . then maybe I should leave them.*

But how he could do that and where he would go was troubling. He tried to remember where he'd last had a safe, warm place to stay and couldn't. He couldn't see back further in the past than a few days ago. Once more the unsettling feeling came to him. *Who am I?* he thought. *What can I remember? Running in the trees, seeing the tent, seeing the beast attack the girl . . . But what before then?* It was all a blur, just shapes, and something terrible that had happened, not too long ago . . .

At least here he was warm and safe. He felt Flora's gaze on him and blushed. He looked away, ears burning, from Simon.

Outside it was warm; heat shimmered off the

pavements. Simon knew the flat was in Fitzrovia, and so took them east towards the museum. He'd been there a lot when they'd lived in Wandsworth. He remembered taking Anna there – she hadn't been at all interested in anything, he remembered, except in some broken shards of pottery, which she'd stared at, entranced. He'd spoken to Francis Weston sometimes about things like that too, when they were down in the South. He was some kind of expert, in archaeology, Simon remembered.

They kept close together, almost in single file, hardly speaking. They came down a street on which shops sold urns and marble statues and coins – the sort of shop that Simon would have loved to spend time in – but they walked straight past.

In front of them, its black railings all but hidden by brightly coloured crowds, rose the white gleaming bulk of the British Museum.

Flora shuddered.

'What's that for?' asked Simon, interested.

'Nothing,' she said. 'I just suddenly remembered being shouted at by Mrs Marsh, that's all. One of my teachers,' she continued, 'who embarrassed me in front of the whole class . . . Anyway, never mind.'

'You don't have to pay?' said Pike as they went up

the steps with difficulty, as streams of people were coming up and down too.

'No,' said Flora, leading them in. Despite the hordes, it was hard not to feel slightly awed by the cavernous entrance hall and its huge glass roof which stretched over them like a net. Simon felt a little thrill of pleasure.

Flora led them on to the antiquities section. Pike was no more or less surprised than he'd been about anything else; in fact, something about the glass roof reminded him of what little he remembered of being at home. Even so, he held on to the back of Simon's shirt – lightly, so that Simon only noticed when they reached the Greece and Rome section, and when he did notice, he said nothing about it.

'It's around here somewhere,' said Flora, as they went past the Elgin Marbles. In the room next to it, a few tourists stood, but it was mostly empty. 'There it is,' she said, pointing to where Simon could see a statue of a man killing a bull, in almost the same pose as they'd seen in the tunnel. He lacked attendants here, though, but Simon still felt a tug of recognition.

There was a young man with curly blond hair standing in front of the statue, gazing raptly at it.

Flora pulled at Simon, and Pike followed like a dog.

'*Mithras slaying a bull*,' said Flora, peering down to read the notice when Pike didn't make any similar movement.

They didn't notice at first that the young man had broken his gaze, and turned to face them. When he started speaking it was in a low whisper that they struggled to hear.

'. . . yes, it's Mithras, of course it's Mithras. You won't have seen him, of course. I don't know if anyone has . . .'

Alert now, Simon took him in. He was wearing a red and white striped shirt and cream trousers. There was something not quite right about him, though, and it took Simon a couple of seconds to realise that it was the fixity of his eyes. They hardly moved. What if he were an agent of the Knight of the Swan? Or even the Knight himself, disguised?

The man gripped Simon by the shoulder. 'Giles. Of course, I should have said. My name is Giles, that's where I should start, isn't it? Giles Cuthbertson. My name's Giles. I should have said, I'm sorry.' His grip was tight, and Simon wriggled slightly.

'Sorry,' said Flora politely, 'but who –'

'I've tried, you see. I saw . . . something. I can't

tell you. Or can I? I followed . . . it . . .'

'Let's go,' said Flora firmly. She pulled Simon free of Giles's hand and led him away.

'No! Wait!' said the man, louder than people usually talk in museums.

'Why?' said Simon.

'I know,' said Giles. His voice rang out into the air and a guard appeared at the door.

'Know what?' asked Simon. He was intrigued. What could this man possibly know?

'Come *on*,' said Flora. 'He's mad!'

'That's what they say. Giles is mad. Giles looks at a statue and stands outside a church all day. He should be in a home. Giles is a traitor to his family, friends, life. Giles, Giles, Giles!'

The guard tutted slightly, but was obviously used to Giles's presence and moved on.

'Know what?' asked Simon again.

Giles paused in mid-flow and was silent.

Flora shrugged and pulled Simon with her. They were three paces away when Giles said, in a voice much lower than he had been using, 'I know how to break the air.'

Flora stopped. Pike looked away from the statue of Mithras.

Simon stepped forwards, once, twice, wary. 'How do you know that?'

'Simon!' hissed Flora, and then instantly remembered that they weren't meant to call each other by their first names.

The shadows around the walls stirred a little more, and Pike sensed one reaching towards them. He shivered and said quietly, 'I think we should leave.'

'Not yet,' said Simon.

They never listen to me, thought Pike. 'I think we should leave,' he said louder. But they made no sign that they'd even heard him.

Simon fumbled in his pockets for Hover, the tiny bird-deer.

'What are you doing?' said Flora. 'Don't show him that!'

'It's the only way. They said we'd be able to tell if someone was a friend.' The little creature was motionless and not giving out any heat.

Giles looked at it. 'I have . . . read about these,' he said. He gently reached out a hand. Simon held his breath.

Giles stroked the bird-deer's nose. There was nothing for a second – a moment which stretched

elastically, its emptiness washing through them like a wave. And then the little bird-deer shook itself, exactly like Raven's spaniel, and trotted around Simon's palm, pushing its little nose into Giles's fingers.

'He likes you,' said Simon.

'Do you trust me now?' said Giles. His voice was urgent. 'Do you trust Giles?'

Simon didn't hesitate before saying, 'Yes.' Flora, convinced too by the deer, agreed, as did Pike.

'Then come with me.'

Break the air. He'd known the words. He must be on our side, thought Simon, *even if he does look mad.*

There was something impressive in his gait, though. He led the three of them – Flora still moving a little reluctantly – into a side corridor lined with glass cases full of artefacts. Bronze helmets shone dully in the light. Here were swords whose last killings had happened centuries before; shields that hadn't been able to defend their bearers; necklaces whose owners had preened when the world was still young.

'I saw, you see, something strange and wonderful,' Giles said, more calmly now, as they walked. 'I told a friend – he thought I was mad. Other worlds! All my life I'd dreamed of exploring this world – I had no idea. No idea! I saw a girl, last year, on the

street – she was . . . enchanting, like some nymph or goddess. I saw her vanish, go through a door in a church in East London. When I followed her in, she wasn't there . . .'

'The Temple of Mithras,' chipped in Flora.

'And I saw you come out of it . . .' said Giles. But I could never get any further . . . I saw her coming in and out, sometimes veiled, sometimes hooded . . .'

Pike shivered.

'Where was she coming from? Her eyes, her face, her lips – she was beautiful. I left my job, my family, my friends. Once I caught up with her just as she slipped through the door, and I caught a glimpse of the statues – the Mithraic ones. It was such a marvel – the bull, the god slaying it. It's called a tauroctony, you know. She looked so beautiful standing by it that I must have made a noise – she turned and saw me, and the door closed. And when I opened it, there was nothing behind it except the church. I never saw her again. I waited, hopefully – I saw you come out, but I didn't see you go in. So I thought you might be able to help me. I followed you . . .'

'Creepy,' said Flora.

'And I heard what you were talking about. I've done a lot of reading over the year.' They stopped at

the end of a corridor in a dingy part of the museum where there was nothing but near-empty cases.

'I read and read and read, looking for anything that might help me. I found no reference to a woman in the Mithras legend. But I did find something about the church, written in the early part of the twentieth century. An account by one of the young divines associated with it. It read like a dream he'd had. A door – the same door, it must have been – and then a different world beyond it, but that world was strange and dark and silver. Here.' He took out of his pocket a small notebook, brown with age. 'He treated it like a joke, but he wrote about it with such care . . . There were three tasks, you see. They were setting them – the people in this kingdom, in this other world – as a game, it seemed, a bit of fun. That's how I came across this.'

Giles pointed dramatically at the smallest case at the very end of the row. There was something in it, hung almost casually on a hook. It was black and like a sort of tube, wider at one end than at the other, and curved gracefully.

'What is it?' said Simon at the same time as Flora said, 'It's a hunting horn. You know, yoicks and all that. Tally-ho!'

'Hunting?' said Simon blankly.

'Well, this is more like a medieval one. They used them to call the hounds and stuff.'

'But this one,' said Giles, 'is from somewhere else. A place I was trying to get to, I think. It's consumed me . . .'

'Jericho,' said Flora quietly.

Giles looked surprised. 'Yes,' he said.

'And the walls came tumbling down,' she explained to Simon.

'I still don't –'

Flora, somewhat impatiently, said, 'My guess is that this horn, when you blow it, is a kind of signal – it probably doesn't actually *break* down walls 'cause who would want their walls to come tumbling down when somebody comes visiting, but I suppose that its frequency or resonance has *some* kind of effect.'

'Break the air,' said Simon.

'That's it.'

'So that's what we need – that horn there?' said Simon.

'Well . . . not exactly,' muttered Giles.

'What do you mean, not exactly?'

'That's not the real horn. It's a replica. The real one is being tested somewhere.'

'Where?'

'Well, that . . . I'm not sure.'

Disappointment flooded through Simon, although how he'd expected to get a horn out of a case in the British Museum hadn't quite crossed his mind yet. Flora sighed. They'd both felt they were getting nearer – only one task left before they could enter this strange other world, this Broken Kingdom, where their siblings were kept against their will. The skin flayed off their bodies into the map that Simon carried so protectively. The land of the dark creatures that flowed and threatened them.

Simon said, 'Is there any way you can get into the – the place without the original horn?'

'I don't know,' said Giles. 'I don't think so, unless you already live there, if you see what I mean. I think she does – my girl, I mean.'

Pike was itching to leave. Things were pressing in on them – he felt them.

'Do you have any clue where the original is?' asked Simon.

'Now that,' said Giles, 'I might be able to help you with. But for now, at least, I think we should go.'

'Finally,' said Pike.

'Sorry,' said Simon. 'But we had to see –'

'Well, let's go now!' Pike insisted. A shadow was reaching its way round the corner, stretching towards them. *Why don't they see it?* he thought.

'Don't run,' said Giles. 'Just walk quickly behind me, as if we're a school group and we've lost the others. Come on, children!' he said loudly, in a teacherly voice.

They clattered back down the corridor. Behind them, the shadow took form, becoming a black-suited woman with blond hair and dark eyes. She tapped after them on high heels.

Giles saw her and spurred on his charges. 'Come on . . .'

They were moving almost at jogging pace now. Another shadow pooled and formed into a man just ahead of them, and they ducked into a passage to their side.

'We'll go out the back,' said Giles.

They sped down some stairs, taking them two – or in Giles's case, three – at a time, nearly running, causing a guard to look their way with interest. They saw the door to the street ahead.

'Once out in the sunlight we'll be better off,' said Simon.

The doors swung open. Into the passage came a young couple who walked past the four of them as if they weren't there. They all relaxed.

And then, against the light of the street, they saw a tall, dark-haired figure come inside. It was the Knight of the Swan.

Chapter Twelve

SWANS
AND WESTON

THE KNIGHT OF the Swan looked taller than when they'd last met, thought Simon, and there was something birdlike about him. It was as if he might suddenly sprout wings and fly away. *Maybe he's more like Raven than I'd realised,* thought Simon. His heart was thudding in his chest, and the four of them automatically formed a circle, back to back.

'Simon. Flora,' said the knight. He smiled. His cheeks were red. 'And . . . you.' He made a gesture towards Pike and Giles. 'You, it's Giles, isn't it? We've been watching you. Hanging around the Temple of Mithras, day in, day out. And what did

you see there, I wonder? What did you find?'

A pair of German tourists came bumbling through the doors. There was a tense silence as the couple, elderly and jacketed in bright orange, slowly edged their way up the stairs, smiling and nodding at the strange little group as they went.

'There's no need to be afraid,' said the knight, taking a step towards them. In certain aspects of the light, Simon saw it seemed as if he were wearing black armour, fitted closely to his body; in others, he looked like an ordinary man wearing a shirt and trousers. 'The thing is,' continued the knight, 'if you just listen to us and give us what you've got, then you can go home and forget about all this.'

'I don't know what you're talking about,' said Flora. 'We're just —'

'Seeing the sights? Of course. That's what teenagers do, isn't it? Out of choice, on a Friday afternoon, *here*?' The red spots on his pale face grew redder; his nostrils quivered. As if in answer to his sarcasm, four men in their late forties, bearing rucksacks and looking as if they were about to climb Everest rather than go to a museum, came through the doors. As they swung shut, Simon felt the summer heat come inside. He was sweating a

little; out of the corner of his eye, he saw Flora was too.

'You know what I'm talking about,' said Mark, sneering a little.

Simon risked a glance at his back. The black-suited woman and another man were standing casually, backs to the wall, but Simon knew they'd be ready to spring if they tried to escape that way.

I'm not going to give it up, thought Simon. *We've come this far. We've gone into a world where everything is strange, and I'm not going to leave it without finding Anna.* He knew that Flora felt the same as she gripped his hand. And he knew that Pike wouldn't leave them. Pike seemed connected to them by an iron rope. And they needed Giles too. He had answers.

They could get out of this. They just had to be quick. They needed the right moment. He whispered to Flora; she passed on his message to Pike. Simon angled his head a little and repeated it to Giles.

'Simon, Flora, if you want your lives to go back to normal, then just give me what you've got and you can go home,' the knight said.

'It won't be normal!' said Simon, forcefully. 'Not without Anna!' There, he'd said it.

'So you do know what I'm talking about,' said the knight, although a slightly odd expression passed over his face when Simon said his sister's name. A disinterested observer might have thought it was sadness. But the knight was not capable of sadness – or at least, he had suppressed that bit of himself long ago – so it could not have been that.

'You don't want to try anything stupid, now, do you?' said the knight, straightening and flexing. He appeared muscled, tighter.

'Why have you got her?' said Simon suddenly. 'Why did you take her? And Johnny? Why did you take them?'

'You called the king. You said the rhyme. You wanted to get rid of your siblings, didn't you?' said the knight. 'Imagine how great it will be to live without them! Your parents will love you all the more. You'll never have to compete for their attention again! Don't tell me it's not what you wanted.'

'Well, I never meant it,' said Simon forcefully.

'You cannot retract now. It is the will of the king.' The knight put a hand to his side and pulled out a sword from a scabbard. It was black as obsidian.

Simon hissed at Flora. 'The sunsword!'

Quickly Flora took it from her belt. It felt good and heavy in her hands. When she unsheathed it, it glowed with heat and light.

Sir Mark smiled. 'Well, that's one of the things we want,' he said. He stepped towards Flora. 'Now I wonder which of us is better at sword fighting? Sir Mark, the Knight of the Swan? Or a sixteen-year-old girl?'

Damn, thought Flora. *I should have taken up fencing.* She was shivering with fear now. The others were still protectively near her but she knew that they were mostly weaponless. Simon had the porcupine spine; Pike would be able to fend for himself – he had a knife, didn't he? Giles, though, he was weak.

The museum doors opened. A party of about twenty or thirty schoolchildren came pouring in, chattering and laughing – girls in headscarves, boys with earrings, eyes bright and mischievous – herded by their teacher who stood by with a set expression on his face.

'Demonstration, is it?' he said to the knight, who had quickly sheathed his sword.

'Now!' said Simon, and they set off calmly, trying not to look as if they were running away. The knight was pressed back against the stone wall, the flow of

schoolchildren in-between him and his prey.

As soon as they were on the street, they ran. Simon saw the knight standing at the exit. He raised a hand in ironic salute, and Simon ran faster.

The knight started walking after them, slowly.

Pike was haring ahead.

'Where shall we go?' shouted Flora.

'To Raven's – they said they had wards, remember? We should be safe there. 'If we can get there in time . . .' said Simon.

They hurried westwards. They came down a quiet street and saw a woman standing at the end of it. Pike said, 'No, not that way,' and Simon saw the woman billow away like smoke.

Pike led them a different way. He could feel the right direction to go, like he could in the woods. He could help them. He could avoid the places where Sir Mark and his helpers would hide. He sniffed like a dog, sensing danger ahead, and changed tack. Simon and Flora ran just behind him, and Giles panted to keep up.

'How much further?' Giles asked.

'Not far now,' called Pike.

They were jogging through Fitzroy Square, into the streets that surround it, and came on to the road

where Raven's flat was. It was deserted. Mostly.

'Home straight,' said Simon.

They stopped dead and Giles caught up with them. 'What's the matter?'

A man and a woman were standing on the doorstep of the flat.

'Oh God,' said Flora.

'Unsheath the sunsword!' said Simon.

'It's OK,' said Pike, quietly. 'They're normal.' He walked up to them. They looked at him, smiled, and let him past. Pike beckoned to the others. Simon fumbled for the key and let them all in. The man and the woman left.

They were inside; they slammed the door; they ran into Raven's flat.

'We don't have much time,' said Giles. 'They could be here any second. Some more dangerous types, I mean.' He flopped down on the sofa, his long body taking up most of it so that the others had to sit on the floor.

Simon unrolled the skin-map. It was blank, once more. Giles sat up, as if he were a puppet and somebody had yanked his strings, and bent down on the floor to read it.

'This looks interesting,' he said. 'What is it made

of?' He felt it and Simon winced. 'Feels like leather.'

'It's skin,' said Flora hurriedly. 'Human skin. From our siblings. They've – been taken.'

'Ah yes,' said Giles, as if that were the most normal thing in the world. 'So how do you activate it?'

'We had to use our blood for the first two tasks,' said Simon.

'And why didn't it work for the third?'

'We don't know.'

'Why don't you try both together?'

Flora and Simon, both thinking it wouldn't make a difference, retrieved the needle and the porcupine spine and pricked their fingers over the map. They wrote, simultaneously, in the little pools of blood, *BREAK THE AIR*.

The map stayed inert.

'Didn't think so,' said Simon.

Then it began to change – much faster and more dizzyingly this time, but with a sense of confusion. It felt to Simon as if the process were somehow wrong.

'The lines are all over the place,' said Flora. 'How are we meant to follow that? It won't stop moving around.'

Giles looked worried. 'Let me have a look.' He picked it up and studied it intently. 'It's strange.'

Pike shifted from foot to foot; his lips trembled. He padded softly up to Giles and, without saying anything, took the map gently between his thumb and forefinger.

In his hands, the map became stable.

Giles looked at him oddly. 'How did you know that would happen?'

'I didn't,' said Pike. 'I just . . . felt it.'

They looked at the skin-map.

Giles' eyes were bright with excitement. 'That's where I thought it was,' he said. The contours of the map had settled and Simon attempted to trace them. 'Wait,' said Giles. 'Try putting it down.'

Simon recognised the place. 'Oh God . . .' he said. 'It's . . .' Of course. It seemed so silly now. Simon had been so worried that it would send them to some remote part of Scotland, some far island, Japan even. But when he looked at it as Pike had held it, he couldn't help but laugh inside. The map showed Limerton and Moreton-on-the-Green. The horn was in Limerton.

Pike put the map down; as soon as he let go it went crazy again.

Simon felt his suspicions rise. 'Who are you?' he said, more forcefully than he had intended.

Pike shivered.

'Simon!' said Flora.

'Who are you? Where did you come from? What are you doing here?'

'I . . . I don't know!'

'How can you not know?'

'I can't . . . I can't remember!'

Simon was standing very close to Pike, his face right in front of him. Flora was poised, ready to restrain either of them as Giles continued to study the map.

'Let's test him.' Simon was gripping the edges of Pike's jacket. It was nylon and slippery. He'd never been so close to Pike before. Simon studied Pike's face intently. He'd lost the faint chubbiness that he'd had when they'd first met – now he looked almost gaunt, the outlines of his cheekbones visible under almost translucent skin.

Pike pushed him back, some vestiges of violence rising in him. 'I helped you!' he shouted.

'But why? How did you know you could fix the map? How come you can feel the shadows before we do?' Simon was breathing fast, his voice thick.

Pike didn't know. Anything much beyond the recent past was a fog. He remembered being in the streets, stealing. He remembered hiding in the forests. He knew how to do things as if he'd done them all his life, but *how* exactly – that was another question.

Simon turned round, and when he faced Pike again he was holding something in his hand. It was Hover, the little bird-deer.

'Touch it,' said Simon.

Flora rushed in-between the two of them.

'Touch it!' repeated Simon.

Pike stood trembling like an aspen in the breeze.

Simon, almost weeping now, screamed out, 'Touch it!'

And then, just as he was about to push past Flora and force Hover into Pike's hand, Giles said, 'I think we need to go.'

The doorbell rang. They all froze.

A voice came through the letterbox. 'Simon! Simon Goldhawk!'

'Oh Christ,' said Simon.

'Guys, quick, come on,' said Flora. 'Giles!'

'I'll deal with this.' Giles went to the door and peered through the peephole. He saw the Knight of

the Swan on the doorstep. Giles turned back without saying anything. 'There's only one thing for it,' he said. 'We've got to run. Now.'

'How?'

Giles pointed upwards. 'It's the only way.'

They clambered up the first flight of stairs whilst Sir Mark was banging on the door below them. They ran blindly into the early evening of a summer day, after a man they'd only just met, from a man who'd tried to get them killed.

Panting they clambered upwards. Giles had taken on new energy. They could hear Mark shouting below.

They reached the final flight of stairs. Giles took them out through a fire escape on to the roof. 'Let me get my bearings . . .' he said. 'Right, yes . . .' He bounded away across the roofs. Chimneys stuck up like mushrooms. The others followed, more gingerly.

'It's not far to where my car is,' he said. 'Just try not to get noticed from below.'

It was blazing in the heat. The sky was almost faultlessly blue. Simon neglected to look around him, or he would have seen, beyond the expanse of paved roof, the streets below.

'Down here,' said Giles and nimbly sprung down

another iron fire escape. His feet echoed loudly on the steps. They all made it, and now Giles was leading them down an alleyway into a covered car park.

'Any sign of him?' shouted Giles.

'Not at all,' Flora called back as they reached a tiny, rusty red car.

'That's yours?

'As I said – family cut me off. Obsession.'

'Just get in,' said Simon.

They all piled in and Giles turned the key in the ignition, but there was only a guttering sound in reply.

Behind them a shadow took shape. It looked to Pike like the snarling beast he'd first seen, the patch of darkness greater than the darkness. He turned to the front and yelled, 'Go!' as the horror of that beast came upon him. Flora and Simon turned and saw it too. Simon felt sick. Flora gripped the sunsword.

Giles turned the key again.

The creature snarled and bared its teeth, its scales and fur all bristling. Simon felt his heart lurch. The thing snuffled and moved from side to side, as if judging which way to launch itself.

Giles swore and twisted the key once more.

From out of the shadows came the Knight of the Swan, his black armour and his pale face looking to Simon almost insanely cold in the heat and confusion. *It's funny what you notice*, thought Simon, as everything around him slowed down, *when you think you're going to die.* He thought the knight looked strangely sad, and even as the black creature hurled itself into the air and the knight drew his sword and Giles managed to start the car, Simon sank into the back seat and found himself half sobbing, with fear and adrenaline. He was held between Flora and Pike whilst Giles drove wildly out of the car park, past the icy Knight of the Swan, back towards the south, back towards Limerton and the place where it had all started.

They drove. It was close to night now. The sky was a washed-out kind of blue, shading into the slate of true night, and they were driving as fast as they dared down the motorway. But there was a car behind them which mirrored their every move, and in it was the Knight of the Swan.

Flora was in the front of Giles's car, her feet twisted together, her teeth biting her lower lip. Pike was beside Simon, glued to the back seat. Car headlights flashed by in the opposite direction. The

knight wasn't gaining on them; to a casual observer it would not look like he was following them, and still less chasing them.

The knight's face was impassive; Simon could see it in the occasional light that flickered over him. They would often lose sight of him, Giles would slip over a roundabout and put on speed, and there would be five, seven, ten minutes without him – and then they'd pull up at a traffic light, and there he would be, patiently behind them, hardly seeming to blink.

'Can't you go faster?' Flora said as they came into some smaller roads.

She looks frightened, thought Simon. Her eyelashes were quivering.

Pike was clutching his fingers together, agitated, always looking behind.

Giles, ignoring a sixty-miles-per-hour sign, pressed down on the accelerator harder. 'This thing can't. It's complaining worse than my granny. Which is apt, as it belonged to her.'

Pike said, 'Look!'

Those who could look, looked, even Giles, momentarily taking his eyes off the road.

Flying on both sides of them with steady, malevolent wing beats was a pair of swans. They

looked at once alien and beautiful, their feathers so white against the gathering night. They flew so close to the car that if the windows had been open, Simon would have been able to touch them. He watched open mouthed, thrilling at their terrible beauty, that wild and strange glint in their black eyes.

Then the one on Simon's side swooped across the windshield, causing Giles to swerve. He headed into the other lane and just managed to wheel back before another car came whooshing past. The swan flapped off. It made a raucous, shrieking noise. The car was shaking. The three children yelped; Giles cursed.

The other swan veered in from the right, bashing into the driver's window and squawking hideously, but Giles managed to keep a steady course.

'Swans,' said Flora uselessly.

The car hurtled through the night. Simon shivered in the back seat. He heard a great rasping shriek, and felt a thud as once more a swan hurled its gorgeous body against the car. This time Giles swerved fully into the right-hand lane. A car's horn sounded wildly, its headlights blinding Simon briefly. *This is it*, he thought, as he felt Giles lose control. He imagined the car mangled, upside down,

himself and the others trapped inside motionless, blood dripping down his face.

But Giles had jerked the car back into its rightful path. A pair of swans flew on either side of them now – strange sentinels, heralds of disaster. Simon was gripping his hands together; he saw the whites of Pike's knuckles, his fast breathing; he saw Flora, head angled so that she could watch the swans on her left. Flying in and out of the streetlamps they sometimes appeared orange, sometimes disappeared in shadow.

They're massing for a final attack, thought Simon. The car veered off the motorway, down a slip road and into a country lane. *Away from everyone else*, thought Simon, catching a glimpse of Giles's wide open eyes in the rear-view mirror.

Simon hadn't seen Mark for four, five minutes, then heard the beat of the swans' wings. They turned, like dancers, in towards the car, a pincer made of feathers.

'Oh Christ,' said Giles.

The swans, clapping their wings and shrieking, launched themselves, dive-bombing the car. They were approaching a sharp bend now; it was impossible to see what was around it. To their right

Simon could see another path leading into a wood. Giles pressed as hard down on the accelerator as he dared.

'Hold on,' he said, and Simon closed his eyes.

He heard the thump as the two swans hit the car from either side.

He heard the screech of wheels as Giles braked.

He felt the car swing round. *We're out of control,* he thought. He pressed his pocket for Hover. He heard the screams of the swans heighten in pitch.

Before he could gather his thoughts, he felt the car right itself; they were travelling smoothly now in a straight line. Simon cautiously opened his eyes.

'Well done!' Flora was saying. She turned back to Simon. 'Short cut,' she said. 'Giles is taking us through the woods. The swans crashed into each other; they've flown off.'

'It'll give us a bit of time,' said Giles. 'They'll be on to us before long, though.'

Simon relaxed a little. He looked through the back window and saw, hovering in the distance, a white form. He wondered suddenly if it was the knight, and then immediately dismissed the thought. *Though I've seen stranger things,* he mused.

'We're almost there,' said Giles. His headlamps

flashed on to a sign and Simon read, *Limerton: six miles.*

'I'm near home,' he said. He'd never really thought of Limerton as home. Home was London; Limerton was just somewhere where they were staying. When he dreamed, it was always his London house that he walked in. The red tiles in the entrance hall. The wooden table in the kitchen. His sister's doll, sitting untouched by her bed.

'We're going to go to the archaeological laboratories. They're attached to the university. Or at least, we're going to go to the house of a man who's working for them,' said Giles.

'And who's that?' asked Simon.

Limerton: four miles, said a sign.

'He's called . . . What's his name again? Flora, will you look in my satchel . . .'

Flora rummaged around and then found a card. 'Is this what you're looking for?'

'Yes, that's it. He's a world expert in such things. He's called Weston. Francis Weston.'

Chapter Thirteen

THE GAME
AT BAY

'HE . . . THAT'S MY neighbour,' said Simon, thinking of the man that Giles said might be able to help them. Francis Weston, taking his dog for a walk. Francis Weston, testing aubergines in the supermarket. Francis Weston, well-respected in the county. The archaeologist.

Giles almost turned round in his seat, then remembered he was driving too fast down a darkened road. 'Why didn't you say?'

'Well, I didn't know!'

'That's good news, then.'

'It is?'

'It means we have a way in.'

'What were you planning to do?'

'I thought we could . . . break in and steal it. Look, we're here now, anyway.'

Giles brought the car to a bumpy halt outside a house. Simon realised that he'd never visited Francis before. He could make out the shape of the house – long, and quite low, and shaped like a sideways L. There were only two lights on. *That's right*, thought Simon. *He's a widower.*

Flora and Pike got out of the car and shut the doors quietly. Francis' house stood alone. A stone courtyard lay in front of it; behind, Simon could smell and hear the sea. *My parents are so near*, he thought. *Just over that field, beyond those trees.*

'So what do we do?' he said. 'It's late. He's probably eating or in bed.'

'Just keep quiet. Simon, you go first. I think the best thing to do is to tell him the truth.'

'What, that we're being chased by swans, and on our way to some weird dimension where my sister is being held captive?'

'Well, since you put it that way . . . Let's just go,' said Giles, and before Simon could stop him, he strode across the courtyard and rang the doorbell. Simon

rushed after and was standing next to him when the door opened on a chain two or three minutes later. Through the crack Simon could see light and warmth. *I could just go home*, he thought. *Maybe the knight was right. I can go back, and my parents won't remember Anna. But I will.*

'Simon?' It was Francis's voice. 'Simon!' He was unfastening the chain, opening the door, grabbing him by the shoulders. The old man's eyes were bright. He was wearing red, baggy cords, a frayed checked shirt, and red slippers. Francis noticed the others behind Simon: Giles, mumbling to himself and twisting his hair; Flora standing upright, seeming to fill out her brother's jacket; and Pike, skulking in the shadows.

'And who are all these people?'

'Don't call my parents,' said Simon.

'And why ever not?' said Francis, his hand on the receiver of the phone in the hall.

'You can't! We haven't got much time,' continued Simon. 'And it won't be any use, anyway . . .'

'Why not?' Francis studied them. 'These are friends of yours?'

'They are. They've helped me. We've come to . . . I can't tell you out here. Please let us in – hurry!'

'Please,' said Flora.

'Mr Weston, sir – or Professor Weston, I should say,' said Giles, 'we've come on a very important matter.'

'Well. You'd better come in, then.' He put down the receiver. Simon came in, and the three others shuffled after him. The hallway suddenly seemed very full. As they went down it towards the source of the light, Simon introduced Giles, Flora and Pike. Francis led them into a sitting room; he'd clearly been studying some papers, which lay fanned around a dark leather armchair.

'*I am the scholar in the dark armchair,*' said Francis. His dog, snoring softly in the corner by the empty fireplace, whimpered.

They all kept silent and Francis sighed. 'Rimbaud. But of course you wouldn't know that, would you? Now sit down, do. You're making me nervous.'

They sat all at the same time. Simon's legs were jittery, a nerve trapped or something, he supposed. His muscles made him shudder up and down.

'So what are you doing out so late? I've got a lot to do and not much time to do it in.'

'At least hear us out,' said Simon. 'Please. It's important.'

'Would you like a drink?' Francis addressed the room expansively. 'A, er, whisky?'

'Water would be nice,' said Simon as Giles said, 'Whisky, please.'

Francis disappeared into the kitchen as the others waited. The room was well-lit, the curtains drawn. Simon noticed a portrait of a woman – Francis's wife, he presumed – above the mantelpiece. There were crossed oars to the right of it, from Francis's university days. A bronze statue, spindly and alien, stood on the mantelpiece itself. The sofas they sat in were deep and uncomfortable; there was no cushion in sight.

'Those papers,' said Giles. He refrained from looking at them as Francis reappeared with a tray on which was a jug of water, a decanter of golden whisky and some tumblers. He put it on the coffee table, on top of some newspapers.

'Help yourselves,' he said.

As Simon, Pike and Flora gulped down the water and Giles sipped at his whisky, Francis said, 'So, then. You'd better explain.'

'Break the air,' said Simon, at the same time as Giles said, 'The horn – the horn you have.'

'Interesting,' said Francis.

What if they're already outside, thought Simon,

right now, massing in the darkness. 'We need to get it –
now,' he said feverishly.

'Those papers,' said Giles. 'I think I know what
they're about. An artefact . . .'

'What kind of artefact?' asked Francis. He tapped
his long, wrinkled fingers on the side of the glass.

'A horn. A hunting horn. But it's not from here. I
mean, it's not from this world . . .'

'What you're talking about seems remarkably
like fantasy to me,' said Francis. 'Remember, I am a
scientist.'

'Please!' said Flora. Her voice carried through the
room, resonating and vibrating. She put her glass
down.

'Listen,' said Pike.

'How do I know you're not all part of some
gang?' said Francis. 'Have you come here to steal
something? You've heard about some of my
collection?'

'No!' said Simon, and then unthinkingly pulled
out Hover. 'Look – I've got to find Anna. This thing
is from the same . . . world as she's in, or the same
kind of world, and we need the horn to get there.
We're being chased . . .'

'By swans!' said Flora.

After she spoke there was a thick silence in which Francis folded his hands together carefully in his lap and moistened his lips.

Pike coughed loudly.

'Do you feel anything?' asked Simon.

'I see no shadows,' said Pike.

'What is he talking about?' said Francis.

Simon put the little bird deer down on the table and unrolled the map from its bundle. 'It – this – brought us here . . .' He showed it to Francis.

'But there's nothing on it!' Francis held his hands out in disbelief. 'I'm going to call your parents now.'

'We need your help! The map led us here – you must have the horn.' Desperate, Simon cast around, saw Pike. 'Pike, come here!'

Pike slouched over and touched the map. Immediately lines formed; they showed Limerton and Francis's house. And at the edge, as usual, was the circle of black and the tiny symbol of the horns.

Francis raised an eyebrow.

Simon stroked Hover's head; it fluttered, woke up and pranced around, shaking a little as if it were annoyed at being disturbed. It trotted into the cup that Simon made with his hands.

'Well, well,' said Francis, peering forwards. 'My

brain says that this is not possible, but my gut says it is happening . . .'

'Now, please, you have to help us!' said Simon.

Francis eyed the room. His dog woke up and began sniffing the air. 'It is true,' he said, 'that I have been given – under the strictest secrecy – an object of strange provenance, so that I can give my expert opinion on it. But I do not think that I will be able to allow such a rag-tag collection of individuals as you access to it, however you heard about it. And whatever marvels you have here, I am sure that there is some other explanation. Now, Simon, I'm calling your parents – and I should call yours too, young lady, and, er, Mr, er Cuthbertson . . .'

'Giles,' said Giles absently. The dog sat up and stiffened, hackles raised.

'I shall expect the police will want to know what exactly you're doing out here with three minors.'

'I'm not a minor!' lied Flora. 'I'm eighteen!'

'You're not, young lady. You hardly look sixteen.'

'Wait,' said Pike. 'I feel it . . .'

'Having a fit, is he?' said Francis. 'He should be in hospital..' He reached for his phone but he needn't have bothered, because at the same moment his dog starting barking wildly, and the window smashed

and a ball of black fury came rushing through.

It was one of the night creatures, the royal hounds, bristling with feathers and scales, its sharp teeth bared. It headed straight for Simon, padding, gathering speed. Simon took up the map and Hover quickly. Francis, staring at the dark creature, leaped to his feet with an alacrity Simon didn't think possible in a man so old, and without speaking he ran to the door.

Giles ripped an oar off the wall and whacked the creature with it as it came towards him. It whimpered, then snarled as Giles ran off after the others. He got through the door just as it hurtled towards him. Flora and Pike were already pushing a table across the door.

'Well then! The horn's in my study, locked up,' panted Francis. 'Come with me.'

He hobbled furiously down the corridor to a door at the end, which he unlocked fumblingly with a large key. The table set against the sitting room door shook. The creature growled its throaty growl.

Francis opened the study door and they all piled in, Francis locking it after them and shooting a bolt across.

'The window!' he said, and Giles and Flora

rushed to pull a bookcase in front of it. Papers fell like swallows.

Francis went to a door in the wall and keyed a code into a pad by its side before tugging it open. It was heavy and slow. There was a large space inside, full of iron boxes. He took one out, carefully.

'I have no idea what is going on,' he said, 'but I can see that we are in danger. From what, I do not know. Some kind of pit bull terrier or something – no doubt to do with your gang. But needs must. And I can't say that I approve of what I am doing, but there we go.'

The sound of a crash signalled that the creature had broken out of the sitting room. A low snarling came from outside the door.

Francis tapped another code into a keypad on the box. It clicked open. He raised the lid. 'There you are.'

It was black as coal, black as the creature that stormed outside, black as the depths of space.

'Take it,' said Francis. 'Take it and take that creature with you. What will happen to me I don't know, but take it. Leave me!'

Simon put his hand out to touch it, expecting a thrill or a surge, but instead felt nothing but coolness. He picked it up. It was light to hold. He could feel the potentiality of its sound.

'You'll need something to wear it with,' said Francis. The snarling outside was growing louder. 'Here, look, take this.' He unhooked a drinking horn from the wall; it had a strap, which he took off and attached to the black horn. 'There. Put it on.'

'Thank you, Francis,' said Simon.

The creature flung itself against the door. The bolt rattled.

'I know where to go,' said Flora.

'So do I,' said Simon. 'I can feel it.'

They both knew. Back to the stone and the ring, back where they'd found the tree and the skin-map, back to where they'd found their fates and now where their fates were taking them. Into the darkness. Into the void.

'Let's go,' said Simon. 'Remember the sunsword! Flora, it's down to you. The rest of you, stand back. Now when I say go, be ready.'

Flora, a grim smile on her face, unsheathed the sword. The room was flooded with brightness as it glowed. She felt the energy of it in her bones. 'I'm ready,' she said.

Simon unbolted the door, caught the key as Francis threw it, put it in the lock, steadied himself. 'Now. One ... two ... three ... Go!'

He opened the door. The black creature propelled itself in, a blurred mess of killer instinct and horror. It turned and saw Pike, Giles and Francis huddled in a corner. As if smiling to itself, it readied itself for attack. Then Flora moved. It sensed the sunsword. Its fur bristled on end – it seemed even bigger, even stranger. It shuffled round to Flora, its hideous eyes gleaming viciously with the flame of the sword. It snarled in challenge. Flora gulped.

It launched itself at her so quickly it was almost over before Simon noticed. A cascade of blood; a hideous scream; a quiet sound of sobbing. Then the flare of the sunsword died down, and Simon saw the tall figure of Flora standing over the creature, her shadow looming up the wall. It had been sliced in two. They watched as it vanished, shrivelling up into nothing, leaving behind only a blackened shape on the floor.

'Now let's go,' said Simon. He ran out into the corridor, ready to face whatever might come at him. Giles, Flora and Pike sprinted after him, and behind them Francis sank to the floor and wept as he hadn't wept since the day his wife died.

Chapter Fourteen

TO

THE DARK TOWER

FLORA HELD THE sunsword out in front of her. The light it gave out was bright, cutting a path through the darkness. Simon was just behind her, his mind now a blade. *Keep going,* he thought, *we'll get there. A couple more hours and we're there.*

He knew that they would have to skirt round the back of his parents' house. There was nothing, or no one, following them – for the moment. They came to the track where he'd first seen the woman on the bird-deer and he hared down it, not caring whether the others were keeping up with him.

He stumbled on a stone, carried on, feeling the

weight of the horn on his shoulder. *Things are funnelling,* he thought, *and I am sliding through them* . . . They were at the field, beyond which lay Simon's cottage, frozen and invisible in its holding place.

Flora was next to him, composed, her face bright in the light of the sunsword. Pike's ghostly face was illuminated further back, and Giles, red-cheeked, reached them and bent over, his hands on his knees. The forest was still, the sky clear, the stars blinking impassively.

'My parents' house,' said Simon. 'The last time I saw Anna – here. Over the field, at the cottage . . .' He was filled with sudden yearning.

'We don't have time,' said Giles brusquely.

Pike shifted, cleared his throat. He could feel the shadows massing, despite their fear of the sunsword. They were at the edge of things, crawling along a chasm the depths of which he couldn't guess. Images were coming to him of tall black towers; of streets full of rushing people; of a cart drawn by something he didn't understand; of a tall, terrible person whose shadow cast a long shape and whose head sprouted a pair of slender, elegant horns . . .

'Quick,' said Pike, and they set off.

The standing stone was, Simon remembered,

about three hours' walk away. Could they make it running in two? They had water and he was now so energised that he didn't even feel that he needed it.

The sunsword kept him moving. In its light he felt as he'd felt with the messengers – as if somehow the light was filling his veins. They were safe within the sphere of the sunsword.

But it was also a beacon.

Pike, running at the edges of the light, felt as if any wrong step would send him into the abyss. *I can keep them protected*, thought Pike. *I can keep off the darkness.*

It was almost midnight when a swan flew low overhead.

'Keep going!' shouted Simon.

Something snarled in the bushes.

They were all of them filled with this curious energy. Simon felt his cheek flaring up; Flora sensed the welt on her leg.

The swan swept over them again, beating its wings loudly. It screamed an unearthly scream. They had come to the stream, now practically a trickle amongst pebbles. They splashed through it. A helicopter whirred above them. *Is it for us?* thought Simon. It turned off into the distance.

Flora stumbled and dropped the sunsword. It flickered. In that second she felt the weight of darkness. She quickly grabbed its hilt and stood upright.

'Everyone OK?'

They nodded and carried on.

Half past midnight. They were almost there. It was just over the rise of the hill, down into the valley, into the woods. The woods. The clearing. The tree. The map of skin. The writing in blood. Blood, skin. *What makes us*, thought Simon. *What makes us, except ourselves.*

Down the hill they ran, Simon with all thought of his self forgotten. Anna was in his mind. And the weight of the horn, and the panting of his friends, and the memory of the bird-deer. The white hart above his father's desk. The girl with the lion's head. The swans. Pike.

Then his heart surged. They were in the clearing. The moon cast a silvered glow on the grass. Like being in a world made of silver.

There was a swan in the centre of the clearing, but it was and it wasn't a swan. It was Sir Mark as a man, Sir Mark as a knight, Sir Mark as a swan. 'You don't have to do this,' he said.

'Quickly!' said Giles. They'd stopped, a few paces away from Sir Mark. 'Do it! Eat the shadow!'

Flora and Simon brought out the spheres from their pockets. There were three little ones left. They consumed one each.

Giles blinked. He could no longer see them. Pike, who could see more than most, saw the edges of them, and he was afraid. Things were tilting.

'Steal the sun!' shouted Giles.

Flora brandished the sunsword and a long stream of light came from it and hit the stone in the middle of the clearing.

The world shifted.

'You don't have to do this,' said the knight again.

Pike's mind was overwhelmed. Cities, cavernous, vast and deep. The sense of knowing. Of imminence. The clarity of it. The obscurity.

'Break the air!' Giles's voice was urgent, bright.

Simon unslung the horn. He was shaking. Flora was holding the sword in her right hand; he was grasping her left.

'Do it,' she said.

Simon put the horn to his lips. And, dauntless, he blew it. The Knight of the Swan reared up, sword raised. The sound of the horn filled the air,

stretching it and shaking it, spreading into the cracks between things. It went into the light and tore it apart, and where it was torn apart there was a black gash. Simon and Flora looked inside the gash and they saw black towers made of glass and roiling streets of people and trees fringed with mad foliage.

'She's there,' said Simon. 'They're in there. Pike, Giles – let's go.' Hand in hand they stepped towards the gash.

'Wait . . .'

They looked back at Pike, back at Giles.

'I can't go in!' shouted Giles at the empty air.

The pair of them went forwards into the darkness, into the knowledge of uncertainty. The gap stood open for a second or two, then shivered, then closed.

And in the world the pair had left, Giles stood alone. He sank to the ground. Where was Pike? *He's run off*, thought Giles, wiping the sweat from his brow. He saw something golden in the bushes – a snake, maybe, coiling away – but no sign of Pike. *That boy*, he thought, *that boy. Who was he?*

The Knight of the Swan regarded Giles blankly. Tall and shining he was, his armour black and bright, his face cold and pale as death.

The knight felt his shoulders shaping themselves into wings. Rough skin was sprouting on his upper legs. He saw Giles slumped, felt the royal hounds slinking about in the darkness. His arms were stretching into feathers.

'It was wrong,' he shouted at the sky. 'Hear me! It was wrong! Now the ground is laid, now the worlds will shake, now the armies of the king will mass. Prepare yourselves. Prepare your troops and know that you will face the end. For it is war!'

The last word turned into a booming squawk. He was all swan now. He arched his neck, hissed, and launched himself into the air. The sound of his wings was like thunder.

Beyond this world, Flora and Simon now stood in the Broken Kingdom. They were amongst dark rocks. Simon unrolled the map. It was empty. He felt in his pockets for Hover, for the bird-deer. It was still there, but it was cold.

Simon couldn't see Flora for the moment. 'Where are you?' he called, and felt her grasp his hand.

'I'm here,' she answered.

'We'll find them,' said Simon, squeezing her fingers between his own.

'We'll find them,' she replied. Her hand was firm and warm.

There was the sound of water rushing nearby. Something like the moon shone above them, illuminating the outline of tall buildings in the distance, dark towers rising into the sky like fingers clutching it. Something moved towards them. Something like a cart. They stood together, alone in chaos, hearts as strong as lions.

And Simon remembered what he'd thought when he'd sat on the beach, on the day that Anna had gone. He'd looked out at the sea and he'd thought, *Take me too. Take me too.* He knew why he'd thought it.

It's because I asked, he thought. *I asked for her to go. I shouted into the night and called for her to go. I wanted her to leave me alone. She was taken. And when I woke up I knew. I knew she'd gone because of me.*

Now I've come to the land of the Broken King. And whatever happens, I'm going to get her back.

Simon set the horn at his side, Flora sheathed the sunsword, and, side by side, they set off into the darkness.

Acknowledgements

Thanks are due to the following people: my agent, Tom Williams; my editor, Martin West; Melissa Hyder for the excellent copy-edit; and all at Troika Books. I am also grateful to all those who either read a draft or offered general support: Memphis Barker, Bobby Christie, Marita Crawley, Sally Gardner, Alice Hart, Lucy Hart, Freddie Martelli, Lucy McMillan-Scott and Catriona Ward.

For
Tatiana von Preussen

Also by Philip Womack

The Other Book
The Liberators

THE
BROKEN
KING